THE NORMAN QUIZQUEST

TIME JUMPER
BOOK 4

HEIDE GOODY

IAIN GRANT

1

The alarm rang and the routine of another day began.

Maddie Waites got up, went to the bathroom, then downstairs to put the kettle on and make Uncle Kevin his morning cup of tea. He liked her to let it stew; she never did. She put the washing on a timer, made a bowl of cereal, took tea, cereal and Kevin's pill box through to the lounge where the old (but not really *that* old) man was already waiting for her in his armchair, in his dressing gown, the TV on in front of him.

"What day is it?" he said, picking up his pills.

Maddie stared blankly. One of the disadvantages of being a time traveller was one seemed to lose track of the days. "I don't know," she said, going back to the kitchen. She pushed her glasses up her nose and consulted her page-per-day diary. "Wednesday!" she called to him.

The tasks for the day included:

. . .

WASHING
   Mrs H
   Work
   Meeting @ Astrid's
   Drying
   Band practice

ALREADY A FULL DAY, and would probably get fuller as it went on. Maddie had somehow assumed one of the perks of being a time traveller would be that she would have plenty of time, as much as she wanted, but it seemed she just spent more of that time dashing backwards and forwards across the days, spreading herself out even more thinly than before.

She went up the road to fetch Mrs Hawkshaw, who sat with Kevin during the week and, as always, found her already waiting behind her front door; as though the woman had no inner private life and simply waited out the dead hours in the space behind her front door until Maddie came to activate her and escort her round to join Kevin.

After barely a minute's conversation, and a fruitless exhortation to Mr H not to clean the house while Maddie was out, Maddie left for work.

She hurried to avoid being late. She could have used the bracelet of what she now regarded as 'time wool' to jump in both space and time to get to work quicker, but she was concerned she was relying on it more and more to do everyday things, nurturing worries about getting psychologically addicted to it, as well as the possible yet unknown dangers of too much time travel. Her rambling, unbidden thoughts reasoned that too much of anything was bad for you. Too much weed made you paranoid. Too much junk food made you fat. She didn't think too much time travel might give you 'time cancer' or anything, but the fact that she'd even managed to concoct the notion of 'time cancer' was bad enough.

She got into her office at Wirkswell town hall to find an extra stack of work in her physical in-tray.

"What's this?" she said.

Two of her colleagues paused in the act of showing each other photographs of their children.

"That's the environmental overflow," said one.

"The what?" said Maddie.

"You know the environmental team on the top floor?"

"Yes?"

"And you know the roof's been leaking recently?"

"I do."

"Well, it's leaked a lot more. Yesterday's rain came through the environmental team office. Right through the suspended ceiling."

"Yes?" said Maddie, but her colleague acted like she'd somehow explained everything so Maddie had to prompt her further. "And this is...?"

"The overflow. Christine has gone off work with stress."

"She always put the mental in environmental," said the other colleague.

"So now they're terribly understaffed and the excess work has been sent to you," continued the first.

"I'm now part of the environment team?" said Maddie.

"Well, this is Parks and Amenities, and I suppose the environment is one of the amenities we all enjoy."

"I should have been told about this before I just had work dumped on me."

"Didn't you see the memo?"

"What memo?"

Maddie found it underneath the great stack of work which had been passed to her. She was now picking up environmental teamwork. She had no idea who Christine was. Maddie never kept track of who was who in the town hall. She felt it better for her mental health to keep all things work at arm's length.

She spent the afternoon working through incidents and reports on fly-tipping, noise complaints, stray dogs and rat-infestations. After spending the morning finding out how one might go about dealing with fly-tipping, noise complaints, stray dogs and rat infestations. By the time her working day was done, she had made considerable inroads into the pile of work, which of course meant she'd not done any of her regular Parks and Amenities stuff.

She left at five. Her colleagues seemed to be still comparing photos of their offspring.

She arrived at Astrid's house to hear raised voices from within. She went round to the side door to find Teasel the cow already waiting there. She was a recent addition to Astrid's garden, and, indeed, had been making a number of her own additions to the back yard during her time in it. Cow pats dotted the closely cropped lawn. Teasel had also been experimentally eating a number of Astrid's flowers and bushes. Maddie suspected Astrid was not a keen gardener and had selected her garden plants purely for ease of care and general hardiness. Teasel had been putting that hardiness to the test.

The cow now stood patiently by the back door as though waiting to be let in.

Maddie rapped on the door. The raised voices ceased.

Maddie gave the cow a nod of greeting. "How's it going, girl?"

Teasel snorted in a sort of '*Yeah, yeah, same old, same old*' way.

Astrid Bohart opened the door. "Ah, she's here at last!" she said.

"At last?"

"Come settle an argument."

"Happily," said Maddie.

2

Astrid urged Maddie inside, raising a firm hand when Teasel tried to follow.

"What's the argument?" said Maddie.

"All I was saying," said Alice from the lounge, "is if we were to throw in some rattling chains and a few 'Wooo! Wooo!'s that will only enhance the startling effect."

"What are 'Wooo! Wooo!'s?" Maddie asked.

Alice Hickenhorn had migrated from the seventeenth century to the twenty-first quite a while back, but it seemed that twenty-first century products had not yet tamed her wild woman hair. Maddie had never said as much to Alice, but the teenager still gave off residual 'crazy witch' vibes.

Alice raised her hands in a classic zombie pose and made ghostly moans.

"She is taken by the idea of us once again trying to frighten that unfortunately named motorcyclist into amending his habits and thus avoid becoming roadkill," said Astrid.

"We're all in favour of that," said Maddie.

When Skid had died under the wheels of a lorry, Maddie, Astrid and Alice had gone back in time and, pretending to be cops with a speed gun, forced him to slow at the critical moment. Sadly, he'd died not long after, smashing through a drystone wall while taking a corner too quickly. Again, they had jumped back in time to try and prevent the crash, only for the damned fool to kill himself a third time while making an unwise overtaking manoeuvre.

"And Alice," Astrid said, "who now clearly has a fondness for *A Christmas Carol*—"

"The Muppet version," said Maddie.

"Of course – now wants us to do a three ghost spooktacular on the idiot biker."

"Ah," said Maddie. "Hence the 'Wooo! Wooo!'s."

"Exactly," said Alice, delighted.

"It's one of the many, many things we need to discuss," Maddie said diplomatically.

"Never a truer word said," Astrid declared and moved over to a flipchart whiteboard she'd set up in the corner.

"Oh, a whiteboard," said Maddie. "You can take the disgraced teacher out of the classroom..."

Astrid had written a bullet-pointed agenda on the whiteboard. There were three items on it, starting with ALICE'S DEPLORABLE LACK OF EDUCATION, and making its way to THAT IDIOT BIKER via THE COW IN THE GARDEN.

"Is this listed in order of importance?" said Maddie, taking a seat.

"Possibly," said Astrid.

"Then I'd like us to add 'time wool' to the agenda."

Astrid regarded the woolly friendship bracelet around her own wrist. "Is that what we're calling it now? I don't like it."

"It is wool. It enables us to leap through time," said Alice. "Time wool is a fitting name."

"It's an embarrassing name," said Astrid. "We don't know whether it is the wool itself which enables us to jump at will from one time to another, or the configuration of the threads."

"We also have Master Burnleigh's woollen tunic," said Alice. "We should add him to the list. We have seen him in my own time and in the eighteenth century. He has the trick of time travel also."

Nodding, Astrid wrote BURNLEIGH? on the whiteboard.

"And time wool," said Maddie.

"What is there to discuss?"

"Well, we don't know anything about the stuff. We're doing all this gallivanting about with unknown technology. Who knows what repercussions there might be. We could be giving ourselves time cancer or something."

"And what is time cancer?" asked Astrid lightly.

"Precisely," said Maddie.

Astrid sighed and added TIME WOOL to the bottom of the agenda.

"What's those words after my name?" asked Alice.

"Alice's deplorable lack of education," said Astrid.

"What does 'deplorable' mean?"

"It feels as though you're very much making my point for

me." Astrid was unable to contain a supercilious little smile as she said it.

"Is it our place to assist Alice with her education?" said Maddie.

Astrid cast out an insistent hand. "If Alice is going to live here in this time she has to fit in. Leaving aside the monstrous task of getting her ID and papers, her charmless naiveté draws attention. She is in dire need of a rounded education, including maths, English, history—"

"History?" Maddie laughed. "Oh, trust you to bring it back round to your ruined career! I don't think Alice needs to know about Harold getting shot in the eye at the Battle of Hastings or Christopher Columbus finding America in order to fit in here."

"Ha! Shows what you know!" spat Astrid. "History is all about understanding our own place in the world. How can Alice fit in if she doesn't understand the world? How can she understand the world if she doesn't understand where we come from and how our current situation came about?"

"Learning can be fun," said Alice, happily.

"A rigorous programme of lessons with literacy, numeracy and frequent testing at its core will do her the world of good."

"Learning can *sometimes* be fun," said Alice, less certainly.

"And for your information," said Astrid, not even trying to hide her smug and superior tone now, "Christopher Columbus did not discover America. Ignoring the native Americans—"

"Should we?" said Maddie, innocently.

"—Ignoring them, Leif Erikson beat him to it by maybe

five hundred years. And there's also considerable doubt whether King Harold was shot in the eye too. So there!"

Maddie nodded, unwilling to be riled by Astrid.

"Well, clearly I'm a poor history student. I should probably blame my old history teacher. Now who was that...?" Maddie pretended to struggle to remember, Astrid scowled bitterly.

3

Astrid had very little respect for the opinions of Alice Hickenhorn and Maddie Waites. One was an out of her time know-nothing too easily led by her heart, while the other was a wilfully wrongheaded and contrary young woman, a rebel without a clue. Nonetheless, just for the sake of an easy life, she agreed that they would indeed make plans to save the biker Skid from his own stupidity one more time, and conceded Maddie was very welcome to conduct whatever researches she wanted into the strange wool, on the proviso she didn't insist on calling it 'time wool'.

Meanwhile Astrid devoted much of the next week to devising a scheme of learning for young Alice that would bring her education up to scratch in the shortest time possible. In many ways it was a refreshing challenge. In Alice she had a student who was unencumbered by any kind of formal education; a young woman who had only learned the skills required to work on her granny's pitiful smallholding and who had been subject to no teachings other than those imparted from the church pulpit.

However, Alice had already discovered the internet via Astrid's laptop and, with what few words she could put together, had begun a haphazard and organic education of her own. The internet being the internet, that education frequently drifted towards cats, pornography and the latest dance crazes. It was a useless, even counter-productive form of self-teaching.

Astrid felt it was imperative she address all this as soon as possible. Alice, despite lodging under Astrid's roof (and thus owing her host some debt of gratitude, surely), seemed less enthusiastic.

The following morning, Astrid was partway through explaining her own pedagogical ethos, her educational philosophy, when the letterbox snapped. Alice leapt up from the breakfast table and went to get the post. The delivery of mail was a novelty Alice enjoyed. Breaking one's fast before completing the chores of the day was a novelty she enjoyed. Sugar-frosted cereals that turned the milk brown or pink or blue were yet further wondrous novelties.

"I was in the middle of explaining my behaviourist approach to education: how the teacher is the single point of authority in the room," Astrid complained as Alice returned.

"This one has a sticky stamp with the king's head on it," said Alice, delighted.

"Yes, yes, very good," said Astrid.

"It is a seal of authority which compels the postman to deliver these letters."

"No, not quite. I'm not sure if King Charles is very big on compelling anyone to do anything. Much more a 'rule by consensus' chap."

"Would he have opinions on witches?"

"I beg your pardon."

"His Majesty King James had strong opinions on witches."

"He, er, did. Yes. Charles..." Astrid considered what she knew about the king. An environmentalist, known to talk to his own plants. "I could imagine he was in favour of them."

"Oh," said Alice. "Not that I'm a witch," she added.

"No."

She flipped over an envelope. "This one does not bear his seal but there are important red letters on it."

"Give it here," said Astrid and quickly opened the official looking letter. "It's from the council."

"The king's council?"

"The town council." She scanned through the paragraphs of bureaucratic waffle. "*Pests and vermin... Noise issues and noxious smells...* Someone's lodged a formal complaint! Against me!"

"You have been accused?"

"Of anti-social behaviour."

"I have met more sociable people...," said Alice carefully.

"It's about your bloody cow!"

"Teasel? She's not a pest or vermin!"

"One of the interfering busybodies round here has—!" Astrid huffed and looked about as though she might be able to see the offending neighbour through the walls of her house. "A woman tries to live a quiet life in peace and this is what happens!"

"Who could be offended by a lovely cow?" said Alice.

"Oh, the cow is an offence all right," said Astrid. "She's a blight on my garden and an embarrassment to have on my property. But the offence and the embarrassment are *mine*. The cow's not in their garden, is it? It's not eating their flowering bushes, is it?" She scowled, enjoying the pleasure one could get from a good scowl. "It will be that sanctimonious git Brian Leadcock at number eight. Oh, he's always acting like he's better than the rest of us."

Astrid snatched up her phone, consulted the letter and dialled the council number.

An automated voice started speaking and she immediately hit the asterisk key. "I want to talk to a human," she said in the slow loud voice she might use to address non-English speakers.

The automated voice tried to offer her options to pick from again, but Astrid repeatedly pressed star until the system gave in.

"Hello, Wirkswell Council parks and amenities," came a woman's voice.

"I've been sent a completely erroneous and unwarranted complaint letter regarding 'vermin' on my premises," said Astrid.

"Oh, you want the environmental team," said the woman.

"Then put me through."

"Oh, that's me too. Hello, Wirkswell Council environmental services team."

Astrid was about to question why the woman had to

introduce herself a second time, as though the call had been transferred, when she realised she knew who the woman was. "Maddie? Is that you?"

"Astrid?"

"Since when do you work on the environmental team?"

"Since the leaky roof drove Christine mad and half their work has been sent down here. Did you say you have vermin at your place?"

"I most certainly do not. I have a cow in my garden and a neighbour who thinks it's permissible to stick their nose in my business."

There was a brief keyboard clickety-clack on the line. *"Ah, yes. A complaint regarding noise and smell. The complainant wasn't sure if they should be reporting vermin or a noisy dog."*

"The cow is neither a rat nor a dog."

"Vermin don't have to be rats. Any number of animals can be classified as vermin. Rats, foxes, pigeons."

"Cows? Really?"

"Teasel is not vermin," agreed Alice vehemently.

"Funnily enough, cow doesn't appear on the tick list on the website form," said Maddie.

"For obvious reasons," said Astrid.

"Yes," said Maddie, slowly. *"And just to be clear, the obvious reason is because we've never had someone trying to keep a cow in their back garden before."*

"It's that git Brian Leadcock, isn't it?"

"You know I can't tell you who made the original complaint."

"Oh, but you can see who the person is, yes?"

Maddie paused. *"I have that information in front of me."*

"It's bloody Brian Leadcock, isn't it?"

Maddie said nothing.

"I sodding well knew it!" Astrid seethed.

"The complaint is legitimate," said Maddie.

"Oh, taking his side are you?"

"Does Maddie hate Teasel too?" said Alice.

"Of course I don't hate her."

"Oh, then she can come live in your back yard."

"No, thank you. I'm merely saying that if an animal is creating noticeable offence, irritation or upset to local residents then an appropriately appointed representative of the council could confiscate the animal and have it destroyed."

"Ha!" Astrid barked. "Let them try! Any pencil-pushing desk-jockey from the council tries to come here, I'll soon show them—" She hesitated. "Would that appointed council representative happen to be you?"

"No," said Maddie, laughing. *"No, it would be— Oh. Um."* She sighed heavily on the line. *"Oh crap."*

4

Although she had a keen idea what form Alice's education should take, Astrid found it easier and much more satisfying to wait for Alice to make some ignorant statement and use that as the basis for the girl's next lessons.

Even something as innocuous as the mentioning of the Sun coming up would give Astrid the pretext to discuss the model of the Solar System and explain how it was in fact the turning of the Earth that caused the appearance of the Sun to rise rather than it actually moving. That kept them busy all Friday morning, including the names of all the planets and several of the moons in the Solar System.

"So, Pluto was not a planet until someone discovered it and then it stopped being a planet after a while because it was too small?" said Alice.

"Correct. Good quiz fact. I think we should enter a pub quiz at some point to test what we've learned. That's some superb colouring in you're doing there," said Astrid. "I'm not sure Neptune should be pink in colour, but it's lovely anyway."

Astrid made sure Alice wrote the names of the planets on her diagram. Her atrocious penmanship was slowly improving.

"And all the planets were made in the Big Bang?" said Alice.

"Yes," said Astrid.

"And what made the Big Bang?"

Astrid wanted to answer the question confidently, because it was something she was sure she should feel confident about. The origins of the Universe was one of those popular science subjects that she enjoyed, just like evolution and chaos theory. She'd read many books on popular science subjects and she'd always come away from them feeling fulfilled, a better person, better educated, and yet ... the specific details did seem to elude her. It was like quantum mechanics. If someone asked her what quantum mechanics was about she would have been able to say it was about very tiny events, involving little quantum particles that were also waves at the same time, and it was all about things being indeterminate – like that cat in the box that was both dead and not dead at the same time.

"Nothing made the Big Bang," said Astrid.

"Nothing?"

"It doesn't have a cause. There was nothing before it."

"There must have been something before it," said Alice.

"No."

"Nothing?"

"Nothing at all. It just happened."

"All by itself, without warning?"

"Correct."

Alice drew back, concerned. "So, like, another one could happen right now, right here." She looked about as though a Big Bang might occur in their vicinity at any moment.

"No. It's really not like that. It's certainly not going to happen in my living room. It needs specific conditions to happen."

"I thought you said it had no cause."

"Well, it doesn't."

"So, it could happen anywhere, any time. In fact, why aren't there Big Bangs going off all the time, everywhere."

"I don't know. It's not important. It's certainly not going to be coming up in any pub quiz questions soon."

"A pub quiz. Is that why you're teaching me this stuff?"

"No, not at all!" insisted Astrid firmly. "It might just be a standard of general knowledge to aim for."

There was a knock at the door. Astrid went and answered it. It was Maddie.

"You're here earlier than normal," said Astrid.

Maddie rolled her eyes, cleared her throat and presented Astrid with her little laminated work ID. "Good morning. I've come from Wirkswell Council environmental team. I'm following up on a letter we sent to you the other day."

Maddie's attempts to sound official were thwarted somewhat by Teasel leaning over her shoulder and gently nuzzling her ear.

"Oh, they've sent you round to harass me, have they?" sighed Astrid.

"I'm not sure there is a 'they'," said Maddie. "The complaint comes in, we have a procedure."

"And this is how totalitarian governments oppress people: with procedures, enforced by little grey bureaucrats who were 'only following orders'," Astrid sneered.

The rhododendron bush looming over the fence from next door's garden quivered though there was no breeze.

Maddie frowned. "Are you comparing Wirkswell Town Council with the Nazis? Our little council. Bin collections, mowing the grass verges, funding the libraries…?"

"Oh, all oppressive systems start out small. You watch."

"I will," said Maddie. "Anyway, we are following up on the complaint regarding nuisance pets kept on your property."

"I thought it was vermin."

"Pets, vermin. Point is – stop, licking my ear, Teasel! – the council wishes to inform you that you cannot keep a cow here."

"It's my land, isn't it?"

"Yes, but—" Maddie consulted the notes she'd brought with her "—you need to have a county parish holding number if you wish to keep livestock on your property."

"A what?"

"Trust me. I had to look it up. If you want to keep cows, pigs, goats, deer, bison or sheep you need one."

"Can we get a pig?" Alice called from inside.

"We are not getting a pig," Astrid growled.

"Morning, Alice!" Maddie called.

"Good morning! We are learning facts for a pub quiz!"

Maddie looked at Astrid. "Are we doing a pub quiz?"

"Not specifically," said Astrid.

"They do a good one up at the Old Schoolhouse on a Thursday."

"A good chance to put Alice's learning to the test," Astrid conceded, then remembered they were discussing official matters. "Well, thank you for coming round, Miss Council Functionary. You've given me your little warning. Now what?"

"What?" said Maddie.

"Yes. Now what?"

"Now, you need to either officially register your land for keeping livestock, which will probably be refused, or you have the cow moved."

"Or?"

"Or...?"

"Yes. What if I don't do any of those other things?"

"You might be fined and the animal could be confiscated and destroyed."

Astrid narrowed her eyes. "I've fought the law before, Miss Waites."

"Have you won?"

Next door's rhododendron bush quivered some more.

"Sometimes, the principle is more important than the victory," said Astrid.

Maddie reached up and scratched the attention-hungry cow's head. "This is a principle, is it? Keeping a cow in your back garden?"

"Tyrants must be resisted at every turn."

Maddie gave her a sad little smile. "Fine. Good. Now, that's done, can I come in for a cuppa?"

"What?" said Astrid.

"I'm parched. And we've got a pub quiz to prepare for apparently. Oh, and I need to tell Alice about these ghostly chains I've found in the charity shop for our Skid Spooktacular."

"Oh, no, no, no," said Astrid, a hand held out to bar Maddie's way. "You have shown your true colours today. No cups of tea for you this morning. In the past, women were tarred and feathered for offering comfort to the enemy."

"Is this a Nazi thing again?" said Maddie.

"If the jackboot fits!"

Maddie wearily stepped back. "I might have been a rubbish history student but even I'm certain the Nazis weren't particularly interested in persecuting cows."

Astrid made a shooing motion. "Begone! Come back when you've taken off the uniform of the enemy."

Maddie tugged at her T-shirt. "These are my regular clothes. You know that, right?"

But Astrid was not one to be swayed and Maddie slunk away, round shoulders sagging.

Astrid turned her attention to the quivering rhododendron.

"I know you're there, Brian Leadcock!" she said loudly. "And I know you put this vexatious complaint to the council."

"Don't know what you're talking about," came a deep voice from the other side of the fence. "Anyone could have put in that complaint."

"They could have, but you did it, you sly weasel of a man."

"I don't know why you're getting grumpy with me, Astrid. The public-spirited person who made the complaint clearly feels something needed to be done about the noises and smells coming from your garden."

"Too scared to face me themselves, eh?" she jeered.

"We pay taxes for a reason," the invisible coward retorted. "Might as well get the council to do the job. I'm surprised you didn't think about the effect it would have on house prices before you moved that beast onto your property. You've always been an irrational woman, Astrid."

"Irrational?" she squeaked.

"Yes. It means illogical. Not level-headed."

"I know what it means, you conceited oik!" she said and slammed the door.

5

Alice was pleased Astrid's anger eased enough over the following days to allow Maddie to come back into the house and help prepare for their mission to save the motorcyclist Skid from his grisly encounter with a delivery vehicle on a roundabout just outside town.

Astrid had also reluctantly permitted Alice to use the whiteboard in the lounge to draw out her plan. Alice had told Astrid it would be an opportunity to show off her increased faculty with letters and she had written out the words OUR QUEST TO SAVE MR SKID in careful handwriting at the top of the board.

Underneath, Alice had drawn a diagram of stick figure people and arrows.

Maddie settled on the sofa with the cup of tea Astrid had grudgingly made for her. "Okay, talk us through ... all this," she said, waving her hand airily.

Astrid sat, hands on knees, staring intently at Alice's presentation.

"This is a representation of us three." Alice pointed to a trio of figures. "We're here, now. Skid died the Friday before last on the road to Tickley. Our plan is to jump back to that Friday, take images of the crash with one of your phone devices and, most importantly, of dead Skid's body and face. Skid must be able to recognise the body as his."

"Filming a traffic accident is creepy and weird," said Maddie.

"Positively ghoulish, but morally acceptable in this case," said Astrid.

"We then jump back two days earlier and in our ghostly guises visit Skid at his home—"

"We know where he lives?"

"He's a Wirkswell resident. I found him on the council system," said Maddie.

"Big Brother at work again," muttered Astrid.

"*We shall visit him* on the Tuesday," said Alice, raising her voice, unwilling to be diverted by their squabbles, "and in our ghostly disguises—" she lifted the carrier bag of ragged sheets and plastic toy chains "—we shall introduce ourselves as ghosts of future times and show him the fate that will befall him if he continues his foolish ways. We jump back to the present day, check the internet for news of his death and, if we are successful, we celebrate." She pointed to the final drawing of three happy smiling stick figure friends dancing a merry jig.

"I don't think it will work," said Astrid.

"Why?" said Maddie.

"Is there a flaw in my plan?" said Alice.

"Flaw? No," said Astrid. "Apart from the fact that you've misspelled 'Tuesday'. It's T-U-E, not T-E-U. It's just a daft plan, relying upon a belief in ghosts and a general naïve credulity on the idiot biker's part."

"You have some suggestions to make then, Mistress Boucher?"

"Oh, goodness me, no. Let us do this, by all means. It will be a valuable learning experience."

Maddie made a doubtful noise. "It sounds like Astrid will need to eat humble pie when we succeed. I suggest we go to the pub quiz at the Old Schoolhouse tonight and the first round of drinks can be on Astrid here."

Astrid made a snooty noise in response. "And if we fail, Maddie will buy the first round of drinks to drown our sorrows."

"Deal!" said Maddie and the two women shook hands on it.

"Good," said Alice. "Then let us go."

Maddie looked startled, as though she hadn't expected them to leave so soon, but she put down her tea and stood up. "No time like the present."

"That's one adage that no longer has any meaning for us," said Astrid.

Alice took hold of each of the other woman's right hands.

"We need to hold hands to jump?" said Astrid. "We've got our own bracelets. We're not children crossing the road together."

"But we cannot guarantee we will jump to the same time and place when apart," said Alice. "Besides, I know the farm at Tickley well, but I do not know this roundabout."

"Very well. The Friday before last. Thirteen days ago." Astrid's features hardened as she concentrated.

Alice did not know how the older woman visualised the pathways through time and space. She had her own methods, but struggled to put them into words.

They jumped.

Alice stumbled as they landed on a pavement amid sounds of shouting. Something collided with her back, sending her staggering. A man looked back in furious surprise.

At the road ahead a lorry was stopped at an angle in the road, with vehicles lining up before and after it. A growing crowd of people were gathered around the scene directly in front of the lorry. Alice could see a shallow dent in the front grille and the scattered glass on the road.

"We are too late," said Maddie. "I mean, only literally. We have arrived later than we should. We should jump back fifteen minutes or something."

"Wait," said Astrid and broke away from them. She moved across the road, between cars forced to stop by the accident, and held up her hands, looking through the square formed by her fingers.

"She thinks she's Steven Spielberg," Maddie muttered, although Alice had no idea who that was.

"Here!" Astrid called, standing by a bin on the far side of the road. "You'd get the best shot from here." She utterly ignored the strange and disgusted looks people about her were throwing her way.

Alice and Maddie crossed the road.

"Fifteen minutes," said Maddie. She grabbed each of their hands and jumped. There was barely any transition. The sky barely flickered. The only key difference was that the traffic on the road was now moving.

Astrid made a viewfinder of her fingers again. "Yes, this will be good. Phone at the ready, Maddie."

Maddie and Astrid started videoing on their phones. Astrid held hers upright; Maddie had hers sideways.

"Maddie said you think you are Steven Spielberg," said Alice.

"Maddie can't name three film directors," said Astrid.

They watched the traffic, Alice listening for the sound of an approaching motorcycle. "I should have a phone too," she said.

"They cost money," said Astrid.

"They are only small."

"Small things cost a lot these days," said Maddie.

"And who would you phone?" said Astrid. "You only know two people in this time."

"Maybe that's because I don't have a phone. Did you ever think of that, huh? And since when did you use it for calling people?"

"Shush. Listen," said Maddie.

Amongst the sound of intermittent cars going by, there was the raw throaty sound of a motorcycle approaching fast. Alice held her tongue as her friends filmed. Here came Skid on his vehicle, travelling much faster than the vehicles around him. And as the cars slowed for the nearby roundabout, he leaned to steer round them, and perhaps seeing too late the wide lorry coming the other way.

The sound was horrible. In this future world, people had produced the means to make sounds that no human should hear, and the impact of man and motorcycle against the unyielding metal frame of the lorry caused Alice to both jump and shudder at once.

Maddie kept recording, but Astrid dashed forward to the accident scene. The lorry driver was emerging from his cabin, ashen and shaking. Other people were warily approaching. Astrid was right in there.

"Should you be removing his helmet?" Alice heard one man ask.

"I need to see his face," Astrid replied.

Alice heard the growing sounds of outrage and argument.

"You sick, sick vulture!" someone spat.

"It's for the greater good," Astrid snapped, marching away.

She was back beside Maddie and Alice.

"All good?" said Maddie.

"I've got the money shot," said Astrid simply. She looked at Alice. "And now back to the past to present this ghostly warning to our target?"

Alice heard the doubt in Astrid's voice. "You think not?"

Astrid spoke lightly. "I would ask you to consider that there exist people who are too stupid to live."

"Really, Astrid?" said Maddie.

"Everyone dies eventually."

"Wow. You are a cheery soul, aren't you?"

"Is that sarcasm?" said Alice.

"Yes," said Maddie. "Now, let's jump back and scare the Dickens out of Skid."

"Dickens. I see what you did there," said Astrid.

Alice grasped their hands.

6

Alice believed in ghosts.

She didn't like discussing this belief with Maddie and Astrid because she had sensed this future age was a sceptical one and people here didn't believe in many things. Alice so dearly wanted to point out to them that she was sceptical as well; that she didn't blame lameness in sheep on mischievous pixies or assume that old women with a bit of wisdom and knowledge of herbs were witches. She was one of the most rational and sceptical people of her time.

But she did believe in ghosts. How could one not believe in ghosts when belief in them was as natural and as obvious as belief in air, as certain as the sun rising tomorrow. Why shouldn't the spirit that motivated and moved a body today not live on after the body had gone the way of all flesh?

Alice believed in ghosts, but she understood that many people in this time did not and that convincing Skid he was being visited by three ghosts might be what Maddie described as a 'tough gig'.

Maddie had jumped them to the front door of a house in Wirkswell.

"This is it?" said Astrid.

Maddie pointed at the covered motorcycle chained up in the tiny front yard. "He's still alive and he's here."

"We have to do this at night," said Alice.

"Do we?"

"Ghosts are always scarier at night." She opened up the carrier bag they'd brought with them and produced three white sheets with ragged and ripped edges, a length of grey plastic chain and a pot of white face paint.

They shrugged into their sheets.

"Your face must look ghostly white," Alice told Maddie.

Maddie dug into the pot with scooping fingers and began to slather the stuff all over her face.

"I'm not putting that cheap rubbish on my face," said Astrid.

"I think you look pale enough already," said Alice.

"You're saying I have no colour to my cheeks?"

"It's a, er, subtle colour," said Alice.

"How's this?" said Maddie. She had daubed it on her cheeks and forehead and her nose.

"You look like you've put on sunscreen," said Astrid. "Like a ghost that's going on holiday."

"How do," said a deliveryman in greeting as he walked past the house with a parcel. "Bit early for Hallowe'en, innit?"

"This is perfectly normal behaviour, sir," said Astrid. "Be about your business."

The deliveryman shrugged and walked on.

"You really don't care what people think of you, do you?" said Maddie.

"I don't believe I do," Astrid agreed.

With much unwanted touching, the make-up was applied and appropriately blended in on Alice and Maddie's faces.

"Very good," said Alice. "Let us jump inside and then jump back to the night before."

A moment later she was on the other side of the front window, in the living room of the house. She beckoned to the others and a moment later they were inside too.

"This house is cleaner than I expected it to be," said Astrid, regarding the soft furnishings and the floral wallpaper.

"It's his parent's house, isn't it?" said Maddie.

"Focus," said Alice. "We are going to travel back to last night and appear as ghostly apparitions before him. I shall rattle my chains and you two will show him the videos of the fate that will befall him if he does not mend his ways."

"Won't he question why ghosts have mobile phones?" said Astrid.

"Many ghosts carry things they possessed in life."

"And the chains?" said Maddie.

"Are forged from my earthly sins, like in the Christmas Carol film."

"So, you're a sinful ghost while we're apparently sinless ghosts with phones?"

"Do not think about it too deeply," said Alice. "If our

pantomime is sufficiently compelling, Skid will not have time to ask such questions."

"Let's just get this over with," said Astrid. "Last night."

She seized the others' hands and jumped. The sky outside flicked from day to night. The TV was now on but silent, and a young man with long lank hair sat slouched on the sofa. He was idly staring at his phone – until the sudden arrival of three women in white bedsheets before him.

He gave a strangled gurgle of alarm and pulled up his feet as though he'd just seen a rat on the floor.

"Skid," intoned Alice in her deepest and most sinister voice, "we are ghosts of the future and have come to share our dire warning with you." She rattled her chains at him.

Skid, wide-eyed, raised his phone. There was a click.

"He's taken our photo," said Maddie.

"Don't worry about it," said Alice. "Skid! We come with grim tidings of your doom—"

He clicked again.

"That's just rude," said Maddie.

"I think it's a reflex," said Astrid.

"Who the fuck are you?" Skid breathed in terrified wonder.

"Look, we can't do the whole routine if he's got photos of us," said Maddie. "If a million ghost hunting videos on YouTube have taught me anything it's that you never get physical evidence of the ghost."

Astrid reached forward and snatched Skid's phone out of his hand.

"Hey," he said. Having his phone robbed from him also seemed to rob him of some of his fear.

"We do over," said Astrid.

"How do we do over?" hissed Maddie.

"Jump to the night before and try again."

"But this still happened."

"Have you seen us before?" Astrid said to Skid.

"What? No."

"See?" Astrid said to the others. "He's not seen us before, so if we jump back to yesterday, he'll see us for the first time and this version will never happen."

"I do not think time travel works like that," said Alice.

"Don't try to overthink it. It makes sense to me."

"It only makes sense because you aren't thinking about it properly."

"What are you?" said Skid.

"Ghosts of future times," said Alice, rattling her chains.

Skid frowned. "Why's she's trying to sound like a man?"

"I'm not."

Astrid tilted her head. "You are a bit. You're trying to do deep and booming portentousness and, no, I don't think it's working."

"Fine," Alice tutted. "Any more acting notes?"

"I mean, I haven't got a fucking clue how you did it," said Skid. "You just appeared. Am I being punked? Is this a prank show?"

"Right," said Maddie, ignoring him. "We jump back twenty-four hours."

They linked hands and jumped.

Skid was no longer on the sofa and had been replaced by a man and woman in their sixties.

"Jesus H Christ!" the man yelled.

The woman dropped the remains of her custard cream in her cup of tea in shock.

"Skid's not here," said Maddie.

"What the bloody hell is this?" demanded the quaking man.

"We are ghosts of future times," said Alice, going for a scratchy and whiny spooky voice this time. "We come with a dire warning—"

"Skid's not here," Maddie repeated. "We've missed him."

"Skid?" said the man and then huffed mightily. "They're friends of our James's, Tracey, playing giddy goats."

"What dire warning?" said the woman.

"It's kind of for Skid," said Alice. "He's going to crash his motorcycle."

"Oh, I knew it!" she said, irritated more than anything else. "We should never have let him get that bike."

"He's twenty-four, Tracey," said the man. "He's an adult. He can do what he likes." He angled his face to the door. "James! James! Get down here!"

"He's not here," said the woman. "He's gone out with his girlfriend."

"He's not got a girlfriend."

"I've seen a picture."

"That's some lingerie model off the internet!"

"Oh, and you'd know!"

"Jump back another day?" whispered Maddie.

"Do over," Astrid nodded.

They jumped.

Another night. Skid was on the sofa again and otherwise alone with his phone.

He gave a startled squeak and recoiled into the sofa. Astrid snatched his phone from him before he could take any pictures.

"Stop looking at porn and listen up!" Maddie snapped.

"I ... I... wasn't," he stammered in fear.

Astrid looked at the phone. "Ugh. He was."

"That's Japanese animation. Many consider it high art," he said.

"Shut up!" scowled Alice, lashing out at him with her chains. "We've got a warning for you. You're going to die."

"We're all going to die," said Astrid. "You need to be specific."

"Just show him the videos."

Maddie already had her phone held out to him. Astrid was close behind with hers.

Skid's eyes flicked from one to the other.

"What is this?"

"It's your death," said Alice. "Less than a week hence."

"And, to be frank, we are tired of saving your squalid little life," said Astrid.

There was the crunch of motorcycle hitting lorry from Maddie's phone and Skid grimaced.

"Listen, I don't know who this is but I'm a skilled rider."

"Look closely," said Astrid.

Skid's face was a mask of grim fascination. "Wait. No. This can't be... This is some deep fake bullshit."

"Look at that face and tell me this isn't true."

"When?" he whispered.

"Within the week."

"You're a crap biker and you're going to kill yourself," said Maddie.

His face struggled to settle into an emotion appropriate to the situation. "Who are you?" he said.

"We told you," said Alice.

"No, that was in the previous attempt," said Maddie.

"You're time travellers, aren't you?" said Skid.

"What?"

"You're from the future. You've come to warn me."

"Yes!" said Astrid.

"This is some sort of *Terminator* John Connor deal, right?" he said.

"Um—" said Maddie.

There was a shiny hopeful light in Skid's eyes now. "You've come to save me for some higher purpose. The future depends on me staying alive, right?"

Alice wasn't sure how to answer that one.

"Things would certainly be better if you avoided killing yourself in a stupid accident," said Astrid.

He nodded eagerly. "Message received and understood."

"Er, good," said Maddie.

"I always knew I was destined for something important."

"Yes – you keep telling yourself that," said Astrid.

Maddie looked from Alice to Astrid. "Are we done here?"

"I believe we are," said Alice.

"No more bikes," said Astrid.

"My parents never liked it," said Skid.

"Bear that in mind too."

Astrid took hold of them and jumped them back home. Daytime. Astrid's house.

"I didn't even get to tell him we're ghosts," said Alice.

"Never mind that," said Maddie, scrolling on her phone. "Question is, did we succeed?"

"And?" said Astrid.

"News stories ... road accident ... bike... No. Not one." She looked up. "Not one. Didn't happen. He's not dead."

Alice gave a yip of delight and swung her chains about. "We did it! A life can be saved!"

"Until the next time he does something stupid," said Astrid, but she clearly had no real heart for cynicism. "Well done, though. Well done."

Maddie flung off her ghostly sheet. "And someone is buying the first round when we go out to celebrate tonight. Beer, quiz, and a general sense of smug self-satisfaction."

"You'll probably want to wash that grease paint off first," Astrid pointed out.

"I don't care," grinned Maddie. "Our team name will be the *Kick-Ass White-Faced Bitches* and we'll slaughter the opposition."

7

The Old Schoolhouse was busy, the pub quiz bringing in a reasonable crowd.

Astrid brought drinks back to the table for the three of them. Astrid was on wine, Alice had a pint of bitter and Maddie had lager.

"This is all right," said Astrid, looking round. "Normally pub quizzes are over-run with teachers, past and present. It's the only viable use of their useless knowledge. But I don't see any familiar faces."

"Maybe all the old teachers are dead," said Alice.

"Or maybe they don't come to a pub in an old school building," said Maddie. "Too many bad memories. Like they'll get horrid flashbacks."

"I can imagine," said Astrid.

Maddie put the quiz sheet on the table. "They wouldn't let us be *Kick-Ass White-Faced Bitches*. The quizmaster said it sounded kinda racist. I put us down as the *History Buffs* instead."

"Is there a history round?"

"Final one."

"Time for you to shine after all the learning we've done this week," Astrid said to Alice.

They clinked their glasses together.

"To a trivial mission accomplished and an idiot's life saved," said Astrid.

Maddie gave a nod and supped her drink. "First round is the picture round."

They looked at the sheet of celebrity pictures. Maddie picked out Billie Eilish, Shawn Mendes, Ava Max and Dua Lipa. Alice identified a further four as PewDiePie, DanTDM, Jenna Marbles and MrBeast.

"Sorry? Who are these people?" asked Astrid. "I thought they were meant to be famous."

"They are," said Maddie.

"Well, I've never heard of them."

Maddie gestured at Alice. "Alice is from the past and has only been here for a couple of weeks. If she knows them then they're probably famous."

"But where are the proper celebrities? The *Top of the Pops* singers? The movie stars?"

"Does anyone go to the movies anymore? Really?" Maddie smiled. "And, you know, I'd give you ten quid right now if you can name someone who's had a number one single in the last ten years."

Astrid blinked and stuck out her bottom lip. "Amy Winehouse?"

Maddie rolled her eyes. "She's been dead longer than ten

years."

"She has not!"

"I think you'll find she has."

Astrid got out her phone so she could prove Maddie's nonsense wrong.

"No phones!" called the quizmaster from across the bar.

"I'm not cheating!" Astrid called back. "I just wanted to check when Amy Winehouse died."

There were immediate shouts from several tables, most declaring her to have died in 2011 or 2012.

"See?" said Maddie.

"A room full of quizzers are not necessarily right," Astrid huffed. "They're probably all idiots."

"Maybe if you could help prove we're not idiots..." said Maddie, tapping the quiz sheet with her pencil.

In the end, Astrid picked out one of the pictures: Nigel Lawson.

"Never heard of him," said Maddie.

"Chancellor of the Exchequer under Margaret Thatcher," said Astrid.

"Ah, yeah. They always put at least one old history one in there."

"It's not historical. It's recent..." Astrid stared blankly. "Am I a time-traveller from the past?"

Maddie considered the notion. "Well, yes. I guess we all are eventually."

Astrid finished her drink quickly and went up to the bar to get another round.

The picture round and the first proper round were soon completed and marked.

The quizmaster read through the scores. "...*Let's Get Quizzical* in third with twenty-five points, *History Buffs* in second with twenty-seven, and the current leaders with twenty-eight points are *No Cows Allowed*. I've been reliably informed that's a reference to bovine cows and isn't a sexist comment."

Astrid's head whirled round and focused on a table across the way where three men sat: sporting two moustaches, two Pringle golfing jumpers, and two sets of spectacles, evenly distributed between them. One gave Astrid a thin and bitter smile.

"Brian bloody Leadcock!" Astrid seethed.

"Who what?" said Alice.

"Over there. Looking as pleased as the cat who got the cream. He's the one who put in the complaint about the cow."

"The man who does not like Teasel?" said Alice. "Which one?"

"The knob with the 'tache."

"Moustache and glasses?"

"No, that's Michael Goole," said Maddie. "Works at the council I think."

"Moustache and stupid jumper," said Astrid. "That's Brian, the bastard."

"Round three," said the quizmaster. "This week, it's on nature."

"Right," said Astrid with tight fury. "We're not letting those wankers beat us. *History Bitches* are going to ground the *No Cows* twats into the earth."

"You know, pub quizzes are meant to be fun," suggested

Maddie.

"What common British plant is otherwise known as wild chervil, mother-die, or Queen Anne's lace?" asked the quizmaster.

"Wild chervil is just cow parsley, isn't it?" said Alice.

"Good, good," hissed Astrid in a venomous voice as though she had just tempted Luke Skywalker over to the Dark Side. "Write that down."

Nine more questions on nature and three further rounds later (fashion, music and famous buildings), and Astrid hadn't let her anger abate one jot.

"Last round now," said Maddie, bringing more drinks to the table.

"We get twenty-five pounds if we win, you know," said Alice.

"There's far more at stake here than that," seethed Astrid, shooting yet more daggers at Brian Leadcock.

"Do you two actually hate each other?" said Maddie.

"He set the council on me!"

"Yes, but do you actually care?"

"You tangle with this cow and you get the horns!"

The teams waited for the final questions. It turned out that they made a good pub quiz team between them. Astrid had the wide general knowledge of an ex schoolteacher who liked to disappear down her own peculiar rabbit holes of research; Maddie had solid knowledge of popular music since the nineteen-sixties; and Alice, being brand new to the twenty-first century, was now a keen consumer of gossip magazines, trashy soaps and reality television, so she cleaned up on celebrity culture.

They stormed through the round. Their team was pretty much neck and neck with the *No Cows Allowed* bunch.

"And now for the final question!" said the quiz master, reading from his tablet. "And it's about the Norman Conquest."

Astrid gave a tiny fist pump. "We got this!"

"For the final question—" the quizmaster gave a dramatic pause to make sure everyone was listening "—please tell me how King Harold was killed at the Battle of Hastings."

Maddie grinned at Astrid. "That one's so easy even I know it."

Astrid wagged a finger. "No. Remember what I said. Don't be duped by the popular myth, Maddie. The old story that he got an arrow in the eye is rubbish. You know that, don't you?"

"What? No! We did it in school. I'm pretty sure it was in your class!"

Astrid gave a dismissive wave. "The curriculum insists teachers should perpetuate some of the most dreadful myths, but the truth of the matter is that Harold was hacked to death with swords."

"But it's in that famous tapestry," said Maddie.

"The Bayeux Tapestry," said Astrid.

"What is the Bayeux Tapestry?" said Alice.

"Well, it isn't actually a tapestry for starters," said Astrid.

Alice's mouth pursed. "You two stopped making sense five minutes ago. Sometimes I think you do it on purpose." She gulped at her drink.

Astrid tutted. "On the tapestry—"

"I thought you said it wasn't a tapestry."

"On the Bayeux Embroidery there are the words 'King Harold is killed' and there's a man with an arrow in his eye. But there's also a man nearby being cut down with a sword. Harold's true cause of death was detailed very clearly by the Bishop of Amiens in his song of the battle."

"Now the crucial thing for this pub quiz," Maddie pointed out, "is not so much that we get the correct answer, but that we get the same answer as the quizmaster has on his tablet. Now, I strongly suggest we write down he was shot in the eye with an arrow."

"Right you are." Astrid scribbled on the paper, then held it up to be collected.

They sipped their drinks and watched while the other teams agonised over previous questions, made sure their team name was at the top of the paper, and mopped up beer which they'd spilled on the sheets. It was a good few minutes before the answers were read out, while the quiz master's assistant tallied the scores on a nearby table.

"Time for the answers!" bellowed the quiz master.

He ran through the questions, and when he came to the final one he held up a hand. "For the final question of that round, I asked you how King Harold met his end at the Battle of Hastings. I expected all of you to get that right. He was of course shot in the eye by an arrow."

"No! No he wasn't!" Astrid yelled. She was on her feet, scarlet spots glowing on her cheeks. "He was hacked to death with swords."

"Settle down, love. Quizmaster's answer is final. Let's get the scores on the doors, shall we?" He went over to confer with his assistant.

"He just called me love and told me to settle down!" seethed Astrid.

"You wrote down the wrong answer, didn't you?" said Maddie. "You disagreed with us and did your own thing. A classic Astrid move."

"I wrote down the right answer!" hissed Astrid.

The quizmaster tapped his microphone to get everyone's attention. "Third place, with seventy points, is *Agatha Quiztie*. Good work guys! In second place, with seventy eight points, is the *History Buffs*. A slightly unfortunate name, given that they got the final question wrong. Hard luck, ladies! And finally, in first place, with seventy nine points, are *No Cows Allowed*. Congratulations! You win the first prize of twenty five pounds."

There was a roar of triumph from the group of winners. As Brian Leadcock walked up to collect the prize, his eyes were fixed on Astrid all the while.

8

Astrid crunched hard on her breakfast cereal, trying to pretend she was extracting maximum goodness from it and not just grinding her teeth in frustration.

She'd stayed up late to find references for Alice and Maddie on the internet, showing them there was significant doubt surrounding the story of Harold's death. Surely, when they realised that she was correct they would stop giving her the cold shoulder? She'd had no apologies or even replies yet. Alice was still upstairs in bed, possibly because she had drunk several pints of the guest bitter, which was stronger than the regular beer.

A banging on the door made Astrid jump. She answered it to find Maddie on the doorstep, her arms folded. She walked straight inside before turning to face Astrid.

"We should go there and have a look. You're going to be

unbearable until we know for sure. More unbearable than usual, I mean."

"Go where?" Astrid said.

"Why are you making so much noise, Maddie?" Alice asked, appearing in her favourite dolphin pyjamas.

"The Battle of Hastings. We should go there and see how Harold dies," said Maddie.

"Go to a battle?" said Alice. "That sounds dangerous. What would we do it for? It's not as if we can take photos as proof and demand our pub quiz money." She frowned. "Can we?"

Astrid put her bowl of cereal on the side. "Go to the Battle of Hastings?"

"Yes. Why not?" Maddie asked. "Harold gets shot in the eye, you apologise for going against the team and promise to be less of a dick in future. Harold gets hacked to death and we acknowledge that we won't doubt you again on historical matters."

Astrid wondered how to address this. While the thought was intriguing, she knew whatever was in Maddie's head was bound to be wrong. "You do know that it's not like a boxing match? You can't just go and watch from the sidelines?"

"From a safe distance then?" said Maddie. "Or turn up the day after and ask people what happened?"

Astrid rolled her eyes.

"Nah, we want bullet proof vests, don't we?" said Alice, poking around in the fridge.

"Bullet proof vests?" Astrid scoffed.

Alice turned to face them both. "So we can get close to

the fighting. I watched *The Wire* and the police use them all the time. I'm surprised you haven't heard of them."

"It's not that we haven't heard of them, Alice," said Astrid. "It's more that the word 'bullet' doesn't really fit in with the whole Battle of Hastings aesthetic."

"Stop being annoying Astrid," said Maddie. "The police have stab vests too, don't they?"

"The police do, yes – but *we don't*. We can't engage in a battle. I saw you when you got a paper cut, Maddie."

"I know you think young people are all useless," said Maddie, "but we are faster learners. I could pick up the skills needed to attend a battle."

"Are you suggesting that I am too old to travel back to a violent scenario?"

"Um." Maddie made a thoughtful huffing sound. "I hadn't meant it quite like that, but it's possibly true."

"You're calling me a chicken."

"What? No I'm not! This is not a playground."

Alice raised a hand. "I'll call her a chicken then. Chicken!" She started to strut around the room making clucking sounds.

"Right, let's do it then," said Astrid. "Playground or not, there is a point to be proven here."

"And what is that point?" Maddie asked.

"It's about exploring our limitations," said Astrid. "Time travel is something we do now, right? So we need to know what's possible. We can't always be dabbling in the easy bits of history. We are probably ill-equipped to blend in if we travel back to eleventh century England. We need to skill up."

"So ... like a bootcamp?" Maddie said with a grin. "Time travellers bootcamp?"

Astrid sighed. "If you must express it in such terms, yes. Such a vulgar term, straight from the movies."

Alice straightened up. "Bootcamp? We climb ropes and run through mud?"

Astrid pointed at Alice. "*That* sort of movie." She sighed. "I meant a more focused attempt to refine our skillset. We should make a list."

A moment later, they were working as a functional team. Alice made tea, Astrid fetched a pad of paper, and Maddie searched on her phone for details on the Battle of Hastings. "Hastings, Hastings... Just checking where it is."

"It's in Sussex," said Astrid. "Opposite France."

"Ooh, I've never been there," said Alice. "I would very much like to go."

"France?"

"Sussex. It sounds foreign and romantic."

Maddie was reading from her phone. "So the Normans came over in boats and walked up the beach?"

"It wouldn't have been like D-Day," said Astrid.

"No. They were going the other way for one thing," said Maddie. "France to England, not England to France."

"Enough with the sarcasm," said Astrid. "What I meant was an invasion would have been a much slower process. Transport and communication was all very much slower. We can probably check the dates, but I believe William's ships would have landed days or weeks ahead of time. They would have established some sort of fortified base before engaging with Harold's forces."

Maddie continued to consult her phone. "Yep, like you said. William's forces got here in September. Then they built a castle. Wow."

"Probably just a little one," said Alice

Maddie looked up. "A little castle would be a hut or a house, surely?"

Both Alice and Maddie turned to Astrid.

"What?"

"What makes a castle a castle?" asked Maddie.

Astrid glared at them. "Is this relevant? You know what this sometimes feels like? Like when the naughty kids in class ask a time-wasting question, knowing I won't be able to resist going on about something, so they can avoid doing any real work.

Maddie looked contrite. "Sorry, Astrid."

"Yeah, sorry Astrid," said Alice. "But what is the answer? What does make a castle a castle? I simply wish to know now."

"Oh, I don't know. It's probably mainly to do with the fact that it was built by a nobleman, and was fortified for battle."

"It says here it was made from wood," said Maddie. "Can a castle be made from wood? I've never seen one."

"Yes it can, and the reason you have never seen one is that wood doesn't last as well as stone. Now can we please get back to the list we want to make?"

"This is all useful background," said Maddie. "It says here that Harold's forces were mostly untrained peasants. William's invading army had loads of archers and cavalry. Huh – so they brought horses with them."

"I see no mention of any women," said Alice, peering over Maddie's shoulder.

"I'm sure there would have been camp followers and water carriers and such—" Astrid felt a sudden nausea sweep over her.

"Are you all right?" said Alice.

"Do you have any periods in your life that you just wish you could blot out?"

"Of course," said Alice.

"I tend to have them on a weekly basis," Maddie admitted.

"Well, up until a minute ago," said Astrid, "I had quite comfortably managed to forget I had a boyfriend, back in the nineties, who was heavily into historical re-enactment."

"Historical re-enactment?" said Alice.

"You had a boyfriend?" said Maddie, disbelievingly.

Astrid fixed her with a hard look. "Is that so hard to imagine, Maddie Waites?"

"Yes?" she suggested.

"I was young once. I'm *still* young. Not even middle-aged—"

"—if you're planning to live to a hundred and twenty."

"—and I have had a number of—" she struggled for the words "—romantic adventures."

Maddie sniggered. "Romantic adventures? What are you? A Mills and Boon character?"

"I've dragged my fair share of individuals into my bed, if you must know. Unfortunately, one of them was a history nerd called Paul Holmfirth, and it wasn't a bed. It was a sleeping bag, and too many of my weekends were sacrificed attending historical re-enactments with him. He got to dress up as an English knight and I was confined to being a water carrier."

"So, there were lots of these water carriers at the battle?" said Maddie.

"Possibly not, but the historical re-enactment society wasn't going to allow gender-bending roles in the re-enactment. It was either water carriers, camp cooks – both of which involved men shouting, 'Fetch me my mead, woman!' – or..."

"Or?" prompted Maddie.

Astrid sighed. "These were soldiers. When they weren't fighting, their needs were simple. I'm sure you can imagine what other women might have been there."

Alice jigged in her seat. "Whores! Pox-riddled whores!"

"We call them sex-workers these days," Maddie pointed out.

"So, if we are to get close to the action as women, then our choices are somewhat limited," said Astrid. "Despite what some revisionist historians might say."

"Yeah," said Maddie slowly, "I'm gonna go out on a limb here and say I don't want to be anyone's skivvy or camp prostitute. If we're going, we're going as men."

"I will note that down," said Astrid, writing on her pad DRESS AND ACT LIKE A MAN. "We will need to learn to act like men."

"I reckon I can do that already," said Alice. She slouched across the floor and grabbed her crotch. "Gerruss some ale will yer, lass?" Then she cackled heartily to herself and carried the tray of tea across to the table.

"Will we be expected to ride horses if we're to pass as soldiers?" said Maddie.

"Depends which side," said Alice. "The Normans had an extensive cavalry."

"So who here can ride a horse?" asked Maddie. "I know I can't."

"Nope," said Astrid.

"You mean ride a horse as in sitting on one?" Alice asked. "Not like this?" She slumped across the table on her stomach.

"No, that's not riding," said Maddie.

"I can't ride a horse then."

"But you're from ... from horse-times. Everything was horses back in your day."

"You think I could afford a horse? You think anyone would let me sit on one?" said Alice.

"Adding it to the list," said Astrid.

RIDE A HORSE

"What about weapons?" said Maddie. "We should learn about them."

"What's to learn?" said Alice. "You stick the sharp end into the other person."

"Hm. No, Maddie has a point. We need to have a basic understanding of weaponry of the period. On the list it goes."

WEAPONS

Alice picked up the pen when Astrid put it down, looked at the list, then added another word in her wobbly beginners handwriting.

BOOTS

Astrid turned and looked at her, then scowled at Maddie.

"See, I knew it was a mistake to go on about bootcamps. You've confused Alice."

"I'm not confused," said Alice. "I know what a bootcamp is. I also know boots are important. If there's one thing I'd miss if I went back to my own time it's – well actually it's probably pornography – but another thing I'd miss is good boots. If you do time travelling in yer flip-flops you'll regret it, that's all I'm saying."

Maddie nodded. "Alice is right. Doc Martens for all of us."

"Fine. We will dress and act like men, but we can permit ourselves decent footwear."

Maddie tapped the list with a finger. "So these other things, how are we going to learn these skills? Being a man, riding a horse, knowing weapons?"

They all thought hard for a moment.

"There's a pony trekking place that goes up on the moor," said Astrid. "We could book ourselves on a trek and get some basics?"

"Good idea," said Maddie.

"The man one," said Alice. "We can find men anywhere we look. We spend a few days observing their ways, then we try it for ourselves."

"What, we go out somewhere and pretend to be men?" Astrid pulled a face.

"Sounds brilliant!" said Maddie.

"Weapons then," sighed Astrid after a strained pause. "That one is a bit trickier."

"I know what we need to do," said Alice. "We make a

pretend person by stuffing clothes full of straw, then we all have a go at stabbing it."

Astrid looked appalled. "I can't work out if this is inspired by some sort of occult practice from when you lived in the seventeenth century or whether you saw it on a film."

"Oh it's definitely the film thing," said Alice.

"So we have a plan?" said Maddie. "We do all those things, then we can go back to the battle of Hastings and see how Harold really died."

There were tentative nods all round.

Maddie's routine now depended on time travel for success. She had no idea how she'd managed when there was only one of her. Now she could zip back and forth to make sure that her Uncle Kevin was cared for, her day job at the council was carried out, and still put in the time to work on her musical career as a bassist.

She occasionally wondered whether this would result in accelerated ageing. Did her skin sustain sun damage from every version of her? Probably. She reasoned that it wouldn't always be like this, and she just had to get through these difficult days in whatever way she could.

Very occasionally Maddie would enjoy the chance to waste some time, even though it was her most precious commodity. Friday was a sunny day, so she took her lunch break from the council offices and went to sit on a wall where she could observe passers-by in the town centre of

Wirkswell. She focused on the way they walked, and especially on the differences between men and women. She tried to form an idea of how she could walk more like a man. Not everybody who passed her walked in a way that seemed distinctive, but one particular man caught her eye. He was in his middle twenties and dressed in a very casual style, as if he was on his way to relax in a pub garden. He moved in a way that Maddie thought she might try to emulate. She stood up and followed him at a discreet distance, trying to time her strides to match his. She looked at the way his shoulders seemed to move up and down, with his arms slightly away from his body. His hips had no sway at all. She concentrated hard and managed to copy all of those things. It made her feet splay slightly as she walked, but when she checked she saw his feet did exactly the same. She cheered herself on as she followed him for a while longer. Then she peeled away and carried on walking without a visual reference. It felt odd, but doable.

"Maddie?"

She spun on the spot, hoping she wasn't being called out as a stalker. It was Gregory, his Byronic flyaway hair doing a flappy dance in the wind, like one of those inflatable men.

"Are you all right?" he said. "You're walking strangely. Are you in pain?"

"No! Not at all, I am fine. I just like to mix it up a bit sometimes. It's good for the spine." She nodded, as if sharing well-known medical advice.

He gave her a weird look. "You saw Flynn's message?"

"What?"

"Band practice is cancelled."

"Oh." Maddie had seen the message, and made a note of it in her diary. After which she had immediately forgotten it.

"Between you and me," said Gregory, stepping closer conspiratorially, "I think he's seeing another band behind our backs."

She frowned. "He's playing with someone else?"

He gave her a look. *"Alice's Demons'* days might be numbered."

Maddie felt that like a solid blow to the chest. She was so busy with life that she paid her music less attention than she should and she was, she knew, a lazy musician. But to even imagine that her band might cease to exist... "No, no, no. Come on. The three of us are good together."

"The three of us are passable together," said Gregory. "Maybe it's time for us all to reconsider our options."

"Dark, dark thoughts," she muttered.

"Speaking of future options..." he said.

"Yes?"

"I got the job."

"What job?"

"The Lambert Waris one."

She remembered. Yes, he'd applied for something. And she'd seen signs up on the road where Skid had one of his fatal crashes. LAMBERT WARIS TECHNICAL. RESEARCH – ENGINEERING – PROGRESS.

"The engineering company," she said.

"It's a research company really. They're planning a big facility here. Actually going to get to use my physics doctorate."

"Dr Gregory. Dr Gregory in da house. Wow.

Congratulations." She punched him on the arm, then awkwardly but fervently put her arms around his chest and hugged him. She pulled back. "*You're* leaving the band too?"

"Whoa. No way, Nelly. Just means I get to earn money doing something legit rather than growing weed. Legit science, not street science."

"Cool." She thought for a moment. "As a scientist, you know about time travel, right?"

"You mean, I've watched Doctor Who?"

"I mean, you know the science of time travel."

He tilted his head. "Physicists who spend too much time talking about time travel kinda get kicked out of Physics Club."

"Time travel is real," she said, realising she was in the process of making a big disclosure to him.

"Er, okay," he said.

"I've travelled through time."

"Right. By which you don't mean like travelling into the future one second per second?"

"No."

"Or you took some ill-advised pills and went on a crazy trip?"

"No. I don't think so."

"You don't think so?"

"Don't get me sucked into a conversation where I'm going to start questioning the basis of all reality."

"The best kind of conversations."

"I'm talking—" She pulled up her sleeve and showed him the woollen friendship bracelet. "This. This bracelet allows me to jump through time."

"The friendship bracelet I gave you."

"Yes. Made from the wool you found in the compost bin."

"And that's time-travelling wool, is it?"

"Well, that's the question," said Maddie. "You're the physics dude. You're going to work in a science lab. Maybe you could, you know…"

"Do physics stuff on your time wool and unlock the secrets of the universe?"

"Yes! That! I call it time wool too! Stick it in your large Hadron spectoscope or whatever and…"

Gregory laughed. "Okay. A: they've not even finished excavating some of the spaces we're going to be using and, B: the first thing I'm going to be doing is not sticking your time wool in my – what was it—?"

"Spectoscope."

"I'm going to be super busy," he said. "Which is a good thing. Doesn't mean I won't have time for the band. I'll always have time for the band. But I'm going to be super busy. Maybe bother me with it in five years' time when I've got my feet under the table and I've actually built my spectrometer."

"Spectoscope. You've not going to do very well if you can't remember the names of things."

"And anyway," he said, gesturing at her bracelet, "sounds like you're going to be super busy going on fabulous jaunts through time."

"I am," said Maddie, surprised to discover how defensive she felt and sounded.

"Off anywhere nice?"

"Battle of Hastings, if you must know."

Gregory nodded solemnly. "Maybe pack a first aid kit?"

"We will. We're currently learning to ride, and working on our swordsmanship."

"Right. You'll need shields too. I think shields were a big part of the look back then."

"I'm remember that for when we do our weapons training, although there aren't many places around here where you can swing a sword without getting funny looks from the neighbours or visits from the police."

He shrugged. "The allotments. They're always so quiet. In fact, there's a scarecrow that could make a good stand-in for — Are you going to fight with the Normans or the English?"

"We're probably planning to stand on the side lines."

"Good shout. But, yeah, feel free to do your historical cosplay up on the allotments. Be loud and frightening. Those stoned crack-foxes have been sniffing round my personal stash again."

"Maybe we will," said Maddie and departed, throwing him a lazy salute while trying not to contemplate a future where their band no longer existed.

10

Astrid, Alice and Maddie agreed they'd bring their 'manly' skills for a test run at the pub.

Astrid wasn't all that fond of spending time in pubs, unless she had a secondary reason for being there, like a quiz. It always seemed like a poor way to spend time, no matter what people said about socialising. Astrid wasn't convinced socialising was a worthwhile activity.

This experiment was a different matter, and she felt as though she should try to assume the identity of the person she was pretending to be, like a method actor.

In preparation, she'd had a dig around for some old clothes in the box bedroom upstairs. She moved aside the two-person camping tent she'd not used in over a decade and shifted a box of electronic cables and unused tools. She was distracted for a full twenty minutes by a box of children's books from her own childhood, including a picture book called *Meet the Cavemen!* by one Ricardo Bushrat, a somewhat fanciful non-fiction volume about prehistoric human society which was nonetheless filled with richly characterful pictures of various proto-humans doing various proto-human things – ranging from hanging out in the African woodlands, to exploring the virgin grasslands of northern Europe, to sticking their spears in a very surprised woolly mammoth.

Forcing herself to move beyond childhood nostalgia, she looked for and found the box she was after. There was a selection of clothes, mostly from a deceased uncle, which she had worn a few times to do mucky garden work. She dressed in grey trousers and an olive tweed jacket, and tucked her hair underneath her uncle's flat cap. Obviously her face was bare of makeup, but she drew in some extra eyebrow hair in case her own looked a bit too shapely.

She had decided her male alter-ego would be named Ricardo, like the author of the children's book. She had no real insights into the personality of Ricardo, but she decided her version liked to visit the pub.

Astrid walked into town, and since 'Ricardo' was a man who enjoyed the pub, she arrived early and ordered a pint. Because Ricardo was comfortable in his own company, propping up the bar.

Maddie came into the pub, dressed in clothes that looked very much like her usual attire. But since they were not especially feminine, Astrid supposed that was fine. Maddie's walk was not her usual one though. She caught Astrid's eye and approached, stepping very self-consciously.

"Why are you walking like Liam Gallagher?" asked Astrid.

"Huh. Maybe it is a bit like that," said Maddie. "I copied it from a guy in the street. Nice hat."

"Your voice needs work," said Astrid. "Here's Alice."

They both turned to see Alice as a man. She had gone out in search of the right outfit, and Astrid hadn't seen her since the morning.

Alice could not resist making a performance of her entrance. She stretched herself in a lazy motion, then waded across the floor as if she was on the ocean floor, wearing lead boots. She had selected a huge, zipped cardigan in thick wool, presumably to disguise her ample bosom, and tucked her hair into a beanie hat. Astrid couldn't decide if she looked more like a scarecrow or a construction worker.

"Who's getting them in then, lads?" Alice asked.

"You've both got such squeaky voices," said Astrid. "Can't you speak in a lower pitch?"

"It's an age thing, Astrid," said Alice. "What's with the weird scribbly eyebrows?"

Both Maddie and Alice peered at Astrid's face. She raised a hand to touch her drawn on eyebrows.

"Aren't they good enough?"

"You can style it out," said Maddie. "This is to practise being men. We don't necessarily have to be stylish or sensible men."

"That much is very clear," said Astrid. "Let's get our drinks and find a table so we can share our experiences so far."

They picked a round, squat table and sat on low stools. They weren't exactly comfortable.

"I'm going to have a go at manspreading," said Maddie.

She opened her legs so wide that she grimaced. "Ouch. I might have pulled something."

"Why do they do that anyway?" said Alice.

"I suppose it's those extra bits down there," said Astrid. "I always get the impression men think they need constant airing."

"Airing?"

"Like if they don't they'll overheat and explode."

"Balls," said Maddie.

"Well, yes," said Astrid.

Maddie considered their general appearances. "I wonder if we might blend in better if we were a little less, um, cartoonish?"

Astrid arched her eyebrows, realising too late the gesture probably underlined what Maddie had just said. Her thought was confirmed by laughter and pointing. She sighed. "What? Does anyone have a mirror so I can see what I look like?"

"No, we don't have mirrors because we're men," said Maddie. "Why not go and look in the gents?"

Astrid froze in horror. She had not contemplated the toilet situation. "In there? But everyone knows that it's horrible."

"It might not be that bad," said Maddie.

Astrid was not convinced. "We were going to discuss our experiences thus far," she said, aiming to steer away from the subject of men's toilets.

Maddie shrugged. "It's been fine. I reckon I've mastered the walk."

"I haven't seen your walk," said Alice. "Show me!"

Maddie walked up to the bar and back again, pretending to inspect the crisps for sale.

"That is very good," said Alice. "You need to teach me. I got on fine once I found something to disguise my tits. I can see that tits are going to make things difficult."

"And you, Astrid?" Maddie asked. "If you cleaned off the eyebrows you would blend in well as a man."

"I think we need beards," said Alice. "Men have beards."

Astrid looked around the bar. "Not many in here have beards."

"But they have razors and soap. And frankly, their faces don't look half as diseased as those of men in the past."

"We could get fake beards," said Maddie.

"Oh, God, and look like bad Father Christmases," said Astrid.

"Proper fake beards, like theatrical stuff."

Astrid shrugged. "Maybe. I think we're doing fine as we are. So, considering the pros, we certainly got served more quickly at the bar."

"We did," said Alice.

"On the side of the cons, we can't use the urinals."

The three of them all turned to look at the gents, as if they could see through the walls.

"I don't think they had urinals in Norman times," said Maddie.

"Yes, but if we're to inhabit the roles then we should be the kind of people who would use urinals if they were available."

"I saw a thing on the internet called a she-wee," said Alice.

Astrid looked at her. "You have settled into twenty-first century life frighteningly quickly, Alice."

"I had a lot of catching up to do. My brain has been an empty sponge, and it turns out you've got all the knowledge I could need in this time. I'm becoming cleverer by the day."

"I agree with the empty sponge bit," said Astrid.

"I don't think we need she-wees," said Maddie. "We're making this harder than it needs to be. I'm sure there are men who are a little more bashful about waving their cocks around in front of each other."

"Not the boys I knew growing up," said Alice.

"Nor me," said Astrid.

"Well, we'll just have to be discreet when it comes to toilet time," said Maddie. "I'm sure it's possible. And speaking of discreet, Gregory suggested we use the allotments for our combat training. Hardly anyone goes up there, really. I think they know it's all going to be sold off at some point."

"Combat training at the allotments tomorrow then," said Astrid. "Drink up, lads."

As she made towards the door, the barman beckoned Astrid over. Suspicious, she stepped closer. The middle aged man made a vague gesture at her appearance and even more vaguely at the toilets.

"It's fine," he said.

"Fine?" she said.

He nodded. "You be you, okay? And you use whatever toilet you feel comfortable with, okay?"

"Um, okay?"

"Everyone should be free to live their most, er, what's the word, *authentic* life, right?"

"Um."

He gestured more broadly at the pub. "A safe space for all people, right? I'm just saying."

Astrid left the pub, a little confused. The others were waiting for her.

"Is it transphobic of us to dress up as men?" she said.

"Are you genuinely asking me that?" said Maddie.

"I think so ... yes."

Maddie gave it consideration. "It would be transphobic to say we *couldn't* dress up as men."

"I'm not sure it's that simple," said Alice.

"Asking ourselves the question is the important first step," said Maddie.

"Is it?" said Astrid.

Maddie nodded, though she didn't look convinced.

11

Alice scuffed the earth with a foot. "I don't know why we couldn't combine the horse riding with the weapons training. They seem like they'd belong together."

The allotments on the hill that backed onto Burnley Manor were deserted. The three of them could hack and slash imaginary enemies to their heart's content without upsetting the locals.

"We can't combine weapons training with horse riding," said Astrid. "We would be thrown right off the pony trek if we tried taking weapons with us."

"People tend to frown on carrying weapons in public these days," said Maddie.

"Nanny state says we can't even carry knives. It's insane!" said Astrid. "What if I want to eat a pickled onion that's too big?"

"Wow, that's compelling, Astrid. You should go and join

the gun lobby in America with arguments like that. You could call it the 'pickled onion amendment." Maddie put her hands on her hips and swept a hand around the open space. Alice could tell Maddie had taken charge of this activity because she had found the venue. "We've got loads of space, and a victim already installed, so let's make the most of it."

The 'victim' was a slightly dilapidated scarecrow standing in the unused plot. Alice thought it interesting that the scarecrow was better dressed than most of the people she'd known in her own time.

Maddie pulled out a roll of tape. "I am going to mark some points on our victim. These are where we will touch him with our weapons." She put lines of tape at the midpoint of each arm, at the top of each thigh, and then a cross where the heart would be.

Alice whooped with anticipation.

Maddie fixed her with a stern look. "Now what we're doing here is trying to get used to handling our weapons, and turning them at the correct angle for an attack."

"Yep. Got that." Alice was desperate to attack the scarecrow.

"We must take care not to use too much force," said Maddie. "If we hack up the scarecrow we'll have to stop and probably end up apologising to someone. It's all about control. We just lightly touch the target each time."

Astrid pouted. "Who died and made you our sergeant major?"

Maddie walked back over to the others. "Weapons then. What have we all been able to rustle up? I've got the biggest knife from our kitchen drawer, and this ceremonial sword from the council's storeroom." She brandished a large sword with faded braid at the handle.

"Why does the council have a ceremonial sword?" asked Astrid.

"I think it was part of a wall plaque that had a coat of arms," said Maddie. "It's been in storage for ages. I don't think anyone will miss it."

"I have a rusty sickle that was in my garden shed when I moved in," said Astrid. She held it up.

"That is only a weapon if we get attacked by wheat," said Alice. She touched the blade. "Even then I think I'd put my money on the wheat."

"Fine! Well what do you have, Alice?"

Alice unrolled a piece of oily canvas and revealed a crude machete. "We had this under the eaves for protection, Merrial and me. Not that it did us any good. I went back and got it."

"So we've all got a weapon. That's good." Maddie picked up her sword. "First thing we'll do is run over to the scarecrow—"

"—He should have a name," said Alice. "Jake is good."

"Er, right. We will each run over to Jake, and touch our weapon on the left arm, then the right arm. Just a touch, mind! Then we run back. We're looking for speed and accuracy, so we will time ourselves." She held up an analogue stopwatch.

"Can we scream and holler as we do it?" asked Alice.

"Yep. Whatever helps."

Astrid went first, after some discussion about which was

the cutting side of a sickle. She ran to Jake and gently tapped one arm after another.

Maddie clicked the stopwatch. "Twelve seconds. Good job. You lost some time from being too close, I think."

"Yes! I need to be a step further back," said Astrid.

Alice went next with the machete. She shouted with incoherent rage and tapped the arm targets with accuracy.

"I make that eleven seconds. Very good," said Maddie. "Take over the stopwatch while I have a go, Astrid."

Maddie ran with her sword and hefted it at both arms in good time. Alice thought it looked heavy to wield.

"What was my time, Astrid?" asked Maddie as she returned, slightly out of breath.

"Which button is it to stop and start? I think I might have messed that up," said Astrid.

After a few more rounds, the three of them began to get a feel for how best to angle their weapons. They swapped so they could experiment with different types of blade.

"Pleeeeease can we stab it now?" Alice asked. "I can do the moving about thing, but I really want to try the stabbing."

"No stabbing the scarecrow!" Maddie said.

"I've got a leg of lamb at home," said Astrid. "I was going to put some garlic and rosemary in it, so we can all have a go at the stabbing. Clean weapons only, mind."

Lamb for dinner. Even after weeks in this strange future time, Alice struggled with the extravagance of their diet. For the vast majority of her life, her diet had consisted of various forms of bread and pottage, with the smallest amount of chicken or game on odd occasions. She had quickly become used to such future ideas as KFC and McDonalds, because what they sold seemed unrecognisable as genuine food. But legs of lamb, actual real and identifiable chunks of animal ... Alice didn't know whether to be thrilled or disgusted at the prospect.

"I am going to go into town before dinner," she said. "There is a costume shop on the high street. I am going to purchase the means of creating beards for us all."

"Fair enough," said Maddie.

Alice looked to Astrid and coughed politely. "I am lacking coin."

Astrid sighed and dug in her uncle's old trousers for her purse.

"One good thing about dressing as men is you get decent pockets." She slapped a ten pound note in Alice's hand. "The sooner you can get your own money the better, young woman."

Alice's hand stayed outstretched. "I am afraid it will cost more than that. I would like to have my own funds, but I will need a bank account and employment. And I can get neither of those without identification papers."

"That's a tough challenge," said Maddie. "Birth certificates, national insurance. It's all tightly sewn up."

"You are a government clerk. Can't you fix things?"

"She's not that kind of government clerk," said Astrid irritably, reluctantly putting another bank note in Alice's hand. "Maddie is the sort who exists to persecute private citizens because they happen to be keeping a friend's cow in their back garden."

Maddie gave Alice a cheery look. "Yep. That's pretty much my purpose in life."

Alice walked down the hill into Wirkswell. The costume and party shop – a whole shop just for costumes and the fripperies for celebrations, Alice marvelled – did indeed have beard materials. It turned out that the glue and false hair for making beards was even more expensive than she thought. She was only able to purchase enough materials to make maybe a beard and a half. It would have to do.

The shopkeeper suggested that Alice find some YouTube tutorials on how to apply the beards. This was all well and good, except Astrid had limited Alice's access to her laptop computer ever since Alice had discovered internet porn and Alice did not own a phone. However, she did know of an ancient but powerful source of information within the town which most people seemed to be utterly unaware of. A place called Wirkswell Library. It had shelves full of books and tables with computers, and several helpful librarians who were only too pleased to help a woman with big questions.

Alice did not have a library card. Once more, her lack of ID papers was a hindrance. But the librarians were happy to assist her as long as she didn't want to remove any books from the building. The librarian, Viv, had helped her locate a big book about theatrical arts with many pages of helpful colour diagrams. Alice (who was mostly limited to looking at pictures on account of her trouble with the written word) was sitting and looking through the book when she realised she knew the suited man working on the computer just along the way.

"Skid?"

He turned to look at her. Alice had had little contact with him during the weeks she'd been here. Turning up at various scenes of accidents while motorcyclist Skid coughed out his final breaths hardly counted as social interaction. But she'd seen him in bars a couple of times, and the transformation that had come over him was significant. His greasy mane of hair was now clean and pulled back into a neat and severe pony-tail. He was clean shaven, and had swapped his baggy T-shirts and leathers for a simple suit, shirt and tie.

He frowned. "Do I know you?"

"Oh, um. I've seen you at a couple of gigs. The Old Schoolhouse."

He nodded in simple acknowledgement. "Yes. That would have been me. I go by James these days."

"James? Not Skid?"

"It was a childish nickname," he said. "I realised ... I was *shown* that I needed to devote myself to something grander. Something bigger than myself."

"Ah."

"All of us have a destiny and sometimes we need to be shown the way."

"That's nice," said Alice, wishing she'd not started the conversation.

"Tell me," he said, leaning a little closer. "Do you believe the future is already written?"

"As in fate?"

"If you will. I've re-enrolled on an on-line uni course, but I find myself distracted by notions of— Do you believe time travel is possible?"

"Er. I'm not sure."

"I wouldn't have believed," he said. "And yet... Do you know Continent Cave near Burnbeck? It's quite famous. A hermit guy lived there in Georgian times. The hermit claimed to have come from the year sixteen-oh-five – I think it was – in the company of a time travelling cow."

"Time travelling cow," said Alice, forcing herself to smile to indicate how nonsensical that sounded.

"I know, crazy," said the former Skid, now James. "Yet there is an account of a witchfinder called Continent Berwick sent by the king to investigate witchcraft in this area who vanished without a trace in sixteen-oh-five. An astounding coincidence."

"Yes," said Alice neutrally, fearing he was going to recognise her at any moment and shout 'You're one of the time-travelling ghosts!'. She wished she knew how to shut down the conversation quicker.

"Time has a path for all of us," said James. "I have a greater destiny awaiting me. The spirits showed me. Maybe you have a great destiny too." He craned his neck to see her book better. She angled it so he could see the pictures. "Theatre. Maybe that is your destiny."

She smiled and nodded and pretended to return to her book. She left the library as swiftly as she could soon after.

12

On Friday evening after work, Astrid found herself sitting on top of a placid pony called Buttercup.

The other ponies, with Alice and Maddie atop one each, were strung out in a line behind her while they were being prepared for their ride in a stable yard.

A woman with a freckled face had helped Astrid into the saddle. She tried to glean further details that might assist them in their trip back to the Norman Invasion.

"Has riding tackle changed much over the years?"

The woman gave her a smile. "I'm thirty four. It's been the same for as long as I can remember."

Astrid couldn't really expect her to know what it would be like in 1066, so she smiled back. "So what muscles do we need when we're riding?"

The woman laughed. "All of them! People assume the rider just sits there on top of the horse, but if you get your core involved, it will be much more efficient. As for mounting and dismounting, you want lots of flexibility."

"Flexibility?" asked Maddie from behind.

Flexibility was one of those ideas like 'five a day' or 'eight hours' sleep' that Astrid imagined Maddie was too young and hip to pay attention to.

"Ham strings, hip flexors ... the usual," said the woman. "It's that or you have to find something to stand on."

Maddie smiled. "Thank you." It was a 'thank you' that implied Maddie was definitely going to be looking for things to stand on.

Twenty minutes later they were all plodding up a lane towards the moor. Astrid was pleased she had a slightly taller pony than Maddie.

"This is most peculiar," she said. "It's the fact that these are sentient beings. I don't need to brake to avoid them crashing into each other. Makes it quite different from driving."

Alice's voice could be heard from behind.

"Is Alice singing to her pony?" asked Maddie. "It sounds a bit ... rude."

Astrid listened for a moment. "I was going to suggest it's a traditional riding song from the seventeenth century, but I don't think they had the word 'todger' in those days."

Astrid risked a look behind, even though she didn't feel all that secure in the saddle. "She looks very comfortable. Wait, has she got a hip flask?"

Maddie also turned to look, making noises that suggested she was equally scared of toppling to the floor as she moved. "Yes it is. I think it's part of her attempt to look more manly."

"And that— No! She's brought that machete with her as well! *Alice!*"

"*Alice!*"

They both stage hissed Alice's name, but she appeared not to hear them. Astrid couldn't decide if she was conducting some sort of immersive study into being a male Norman cavalier, or just having fun. Alice continued to sing bawdy songs, swig from a hip flask, and wave the machete in lazy arcs.

"We need to go back and make her stop!"

"Yes. Yes we do," said Maddie. "How do we do that?"

Astrid looked down at her horse. "Turn!" she commanded. "Go left! Or right! Go backwards!" She made clicking noises, but the horse plodded on, following the one in front. "You try, Maddie!"

Maddie didn't seem to have any more idea how to make her horse change direction. She yelled "Yee-haw!" and snapped the reins, then tried leaning, as if she were steering a motorbike. Neither worked.

Nothing worked. Maddie and Astrid continued as captives on their relentlessly placid ponies, while Alice rollicked noisily behind them on a pony which barely seemed to register her presence as she took practise swings with the machete.

It took no more than ten minutes for their ride to be brought to a decisive end. Ponies were brought to a halt. Astrid, Maddie and Alice were swiftly forced to dismount, then the pony trek went on without them. Well-behaved pony trekkers gave them embarrassed and holier-than-thou looks as they continued up the hill without them.

The three women trudged back down the hill on foot, resentment simmering off each one.

"You are the worst kind of blithering idiot," Astrid seethed at Alice.

"The worst kind?" said Alice, wounded.

"Ignorant, foolish, illiterate, disobedient."

"'Recklessly endangering others'," quoted Maddie. "That's what the woman said."

"Not true!" said Alice. "I was only *practising* recklessly endangering others. There's a difference!"

"'Flouting our policy on alcohol' and 'unsuitable and explicit outbursts'," Astrid continued.

"So in summary, they don't suspect we are time travellers in training?" Alice said thoughtfully.

"What?"

"They just think that I am bad and possibly stupid?"

"Yes?" said Maddie.

Alice gave a small bow. "I believe we call that 'taking one for the team'. So I have learned that when on horseback, the hefting of a weapon will swing your weight more than you expect. You need to shift in the saddle to compensate. Another lesson learned. You're welcome!"

Maddie and Astrid exchanged a look.

"No, no, wait," said Astrid, feeling her anger rise further because Alice refused to accept responsibility. "This was a bad thing!"

"I don't think so," said Alice blithely.

"No, you do this," Astrid insisted. "You act all moral and lovely much of the time. 'Oh, look at my knowledge of herbs and my flaky folk wisdom and my can-do attitude to household chores'. But really you're a very selfish girl at times."

"Selfish?"

"You eat my food and live in my house and pay no rent."

"I have no money!"

"You don't get a job."

"I have no special numbers to show the clerks, Astrid!"

"And then you go and do some mind-boggling stupid things like this!"

"*One* thing! In the name of research!"

"It's not one thing! It's ... it's— I try to educate you and you show no appreciation!"

"You are a harsh teacher, Mistress Bohart!

"And you brought a cow from the past to live in my garden!"

"I couldn't abandon her!"

"No! You foisted her on me instead!"

"Ah, speaking of which," said Maddie, fishing around inside her jacket. She produced a letter in a white envelope. Astrid recognised the franking marks and snatched it from Maddie, tearing it open.

Her eyes scanned the page. "*Council inspection ... a fine of up to one thousand pounds...*"

"If you had responded to the initial letter within a timely framework," suggested Maddie.

"I've been busy!" Astrid snapped. "Trying to knock some common sense into this numbskull! Maintaining a house that is increasingly being used as a drop-in centre for bored time travellers! I haven't had time to deal with petty council bureaucrats!"

"You're a time traveller. Of course you have time."

Astrid screeched in fury. There is nothing worse one can do to a furious person than calmly and sensibly undermine every reason for their anger.

"You don't understand—!" Astrid yelled, and suddenly, unexpectedly, she was somewhere else.

Without meaning to jump, without any conscious – or even unconscious – realisation that she had made the decision to jump, she was very clearly somewhere else.

"What the hell?"

She looked about just in case someone had jumped her here, dragged her along to this place. But there was no one around.

"Well done, brain," she tutted to herself, finding no one to blame but herself.

Astrid stood in knee-high grass, lush and green, beneath a bright sky that suggested it was morning and perhaps somewhere close to summer in this corner of the world. The grasslands stretched on for a huge distance, a mile or more, before they sloped down to the edge of a vast forest of deciduous trees. The trees looked northern European; British even.

Astrid turned round and tried to place this landscape. It had a certain aspect which reminded her of the countryside around Wirkswell, but it was too vast, with no roads, no pylons, no building or drystone walls to divide it up.

"I mean, it's really beautiful," she said to herself. "There is that."

It was the antithesis of the chaos and irritation and noise of her day-to-day life. If her subconscious mind had decided to drag her away from the two stupid women who had latched onto her and brought their mountains of problems with them, then it had made a truly magnificent choice.

"But I'd best get back," she told this place, then hesitated. She didn't need to get back. Not yet. Maddie was right on one point. As a time traveller, Astrid should never be able to complain she didn't have time. The one thing she absolutely *did* have was time.

"I don't need to get back," she told the world and promptly sat down to make the point.

Eventually, she would get hungry or sleepy and, out of necessity, she would have to jump home for food. But right now she didn't have to go anywhere.

The wind blew around her, not cold and unpleasant, but a notable presence. Astrid bunched up her coat collar around her shoulders and listened to the wind, watching it sculpt wave-like patterns in the thick blades of grass further down the hill.

She didn't know how long she sat there and she didn't care. Astrid didn't hold with any of that yoga-meditation-mindfulness claptrap, but she was happy to let the raw emptiness of the place drain away her annoyance; feel the wind carry it away from her.

Goodbye, irritation at Alice's selfishly drunken antics.

Farewell, the general ingratitude of the Stuart-era teenager living under her roof.

Ta-ra, Maddie's rude disbelief that Astrid was once young, sexual and desirable.

Begone, unnecessary worries about a cow that wasn't even hers.

Off went all her worries, out across the grass and into the trees. She could picture them snagging on branches, maybe slapping an unsuspecting squirrel in the face. Let the rodents of the forest deal with her own mountain of unresolved dissatisfaction.

When she was undeniably hungry and in need of the toilet, Astrid stood. She stood and took a good look at the idyllic landscape. She wanted to remember it so she could jump back here, whenever and wherever this was.

13

After giving Teasel a bit of a fuss in the garden, Alice unlocked Astrid's back door and held it for Maddie to go through first. Maddie gave a loud 'Oh!' of surprise.

"You all right?" said Alice.

"She's here!"

Maddie was right. Astrid was here, in her own home, and seemed to be going about the business of making a pot of tea and putting out a plate of biscuits.

"So, you just jumped home?" said Maddie.

"I took a detour. Quite a bit of a detour. Which was nice."

Alice noted that the older woman was of a much, much calmer demeanour than when she had abruptly departed from the hillside an hour earlier.

Alice's head ached from the spirits she'd drunk whilst riding, and the walk home had given her time to reflect as well. Her reflections had not changed her opinion on the valuable lessons learned whilst drinking, riding and swinging a machete around, but they had given her pause to think about how much Astrid had put herself out by allowing Alice into her home.

"I think I should apologise," she said.

Astrid immediately waved it away. "Pish posh, water under the bridge. I think we should run through our kit. I believe we've done as much preparation for our Norman adventure as we reasonably can."

She carried the tea things through to the lounge. Alice saw she had heaped some gear on the coffee table.

"Each of us has a disgusting hessian tunic," said Astrid, "which is long enough to disguise the slightly comfier modern clothes underneath, along with these possibly quite dodgy stab vests we bought online. We all have Doc Marten boots and two pairs of woollen socks."

"Wool will be hot on our feet," said Maddie. "It should be warm when we get to Hastings."

"You will just have to cope, Maddie. Wool is our best bet for lasting a few days: drying if it gets wet while looking as if it fits in." Astrid glanced back at her list. "We each have a tiny first aid kit, which must stay hidden, along with our penknives and sanitary towels. Our plan is for a very swift visit, in and out. We will arrive towards the end of the battle, which is when we know Harold meets his end. We turn up, keep our heads down, and observe for probably no more than an hour before returning."

"But we're not taking a watch?" asked Alice.

"No watches. No jewellery – unless it's gold and we are prepared to trade it."

"What about headgear?" asked Maddie.

"Headgear?"

"Helmets. Aren't we going to try to blend in with the soldiers?"

"It was going to be my suggestion that we, er, get some when we arrive. I expect there will be spares," said Astrid.

Maddie's eyes narrowed. "You're talking about looting the dead, aren't you?"

"I am. Make sure you take one that looks like it belongs on the winning side."

Maddie looked as if she was going to say something further, but Alice had something to add. "I want to make us beards."

"I thought we said no to beards," said Astrid.

"But I bought the makings of beards from the costume shop anyway."

Astrid looked like she was going to object, but whatever calm she seemed to have gained since the outburst on the hillside still held sway.

"Very well," said Astrid. "You may provide us with some light beards. But proper ones. Realistic ones. I don't want you making me look like Fu Manchu."

"Who's Fu Manchu?" Alice asked Maddie.

"No idea," said Maddie.

"We're going then?" said Astrid once she had her wispy beard glued in place. "Weapons ready?" She adopted what she possibly thought was a dynamic defensive stance.

They all brandished their weapons of choice, with the unspoken wish that they would not need to use them.

"So we arrive at the end of the day when things should be

winding down," said Maddie. "If it looks really, really bad then we jump straight out again, yeah?"

They nodded, held hands and jumped.

Alice's feet were suddenly slipping in mud. She looked down. The ground was slick with blood.

"Holy Christ!" she said. "Are we too late?"

It was a ghastly scene. The bodies surrounding them seemed to blend into the landscape. Alice had seen dead bodies before, plenty of them, but not so many, and not all at once.

"Brownie points to us for definitely landing in the Battle of Hastings at first attempt," said Maddie grimly.

The landscape might have been distant Sussex, but to Alice's eyes, it didn't look much different to the fields of home. To their left a hill rose to a line of trees. The ground near to them was grassy and boggy. Alice's feet were already getting wet.

"I can hear fighting," said Maddie, pointing. "I assume it's fighting, anyway."

"All that screaming and shouting?" said Astrid. "Probably."

"It's coming from over there, towards the hill."

The view was obscured by a small pool with scrubby willow trees on its banks.

Alice stooped to look at a body. "Did they all die in battle? This one here looks like he had the pox."

"If he was ill he might have died in the early stages of the battle," said Astrid.

"Poor soul. I'll say a few words," said Alice, and knelt down by the body.

"If you do that for every dead person we'll never see anything," hissed Astrid.

"How about we do it at the end?" Maddie suggested. "You can say a few words for all of the people who lost their lives."

Alice looked troubled to be leaving this particular soldier, but nodded in agreement.

"Are these soldiers French or English?" Maddie asked.

"Um." Astrid looked down at the bodies. "It's not as easy to tell as the books would have you believe. Harold's men all wielded battle axes, according to accounts of the time." She picked up a metal axe. "Here's one, but is it enough to prove these are all English? This one here has a bent knife which makes my sickle look good."

"Crazy that they all dressed the same," said Maddie. "No uniforms. How on earth do you make sure you don't kill the wrong person?"

Astrid shrugged. "I expect mistakes were probably made."

Alice picked up a helmet and tried it for size. The nose piece came right down her face, almost to her chin. Her eyes were totally covered. "This smells funny."

"I'd take it off if I were you. You might catch something nasty," said Astrid.

Alice pulled it up off her head with some difficulty and they moved cautiously in the direction of the fighting, jumping over the small stream which fed the pool. After a minute they were able to see across a shallow valley where fighting was definitely taking place.

"So many men," said Alice.

"I was thinking there were so few," said Astrid.

"At least five thousand men down there," said Maddie.

"You count quickly," said Alice.

Maddie sniffed. "My school had a thousand students. That looks like at least five school sports days side by side."

"Hardly a sports day," said Astrid.

Down in the valley there was a confusion of men and horses. A filthy mess of a battle. They yelled and stabbed at each other in semi-delirious exhaustion. There were banners and standards among the melee, but they were ragged and filthy as well.

"Oh, a horse has gone lame!" said Alice.

"Hundreds dead and she spots the one wounded animal," tutted Astrid.

"At least it's alive," said Maddie, then yelled in protest as Alice ran towards it.

"We're putting ourselves at risk!" shouted Astrid, angrily.

"I just need to help!" Alice shouted back.

"Help a horse that died centuries ago?"

Something thudded softly into the ground, not five feet from Alice's feet. There was another thud. She looked at the quivering arrows jutting from the ground.

"Shields!" yelled Maddie, still some distance behind.

Alice scouted around for a soldier who had no further use of his shield and dragged it out from beneath his body. She could see Astrid and Maddie doing likewise. In the shadow of her long, tear-shaped shield, she edged forward again.

More arrows fell. Several pierced the already dead, but none struck Alice's shield.

The roan horse was struggling beneath the weight of

several men laid across its legs. There were no actual visible wounds. The poor beast was frantic with fear, her black eyes wide and darting. Eventually, Astrid and Maddie caught up.

"Cover me," said Alice. As Maddie and Astrid set up a miniature shield wall in front of her, she knelt to tend to the horse.

Alice pulled out her leather pouch. "Here we are, horsey," she said in a calming voice.

"She's talking to it!" Astrid snapped as an arrow slammed into her shield.

"Lucky for you I have some hedge-nettle and some yarrow. Yum, yum. We're going to get you out of here."

Alice worked to pull the Frenchmen off the horse's legs.

"That's better isn't it, you beauty," she said.

Soon enough, she was coaxing the horse to its feet.

"Come on. We'll get you away from these arrows."

"You do know that some local is just going to come and steal her the second our backs are turned, don't you?" Astrid shouted at Alice.

"Nah, I know just the place for her to rest up," said Alice. She put her arms around the horse's neck and jumped, the battle vanishing from around her in an instant.

14

Maddie stared at the spot where Alice and the horse had been.

Less than an hour ago they had all been in Astrid's lounge, discussing equipment. Now here she was, crouching behind a stolen shield, in what was essentially a little hollow in the layers of battle dead.

She looked at Astrid, similarly cowering next to her. "Would it be really silly to say I didn't expect it to be like this?"

"I know what you mean," said Astrid. "I mean this is all quite thrilling, but not in a good way."

"Understatement."

"I think Ricardo is not naturally a fighting man."

"Who's Ricardo?" said Maddie.

"Me," said Astrid, pointing at her now muddy false beard. "Ricardo Bushrat."

"Ah, really getting into character." There was an iron tang

in the air, the smell of blood. "I can't help feeling that all that learning to walk like a man and what have you is a bit superfluous now."

Astrid nodded. "At this point, we could have just come into the battle dressed as our regular selves and everyone would have been too frazzled to bat an eyelid."

"You're right. Frazzled. That word doesn't get used enough in relation to the Battle of Hastings."

Astrid peered cautiously over the top of her shield.

"Careful!" said Maddie.

"I think it's easing up. Besides, my knees can't take all this crouching."

They both rose and indeed it seemed the assault of arrows had stopped.

"I read that the Normans ran out of arrows," said Astrid.

"Is that true or is it wishful thinking?"

"The English didn't have many archers and the French were relying on being able to shoot some of the English arrows back at them."

"That sounds made up."

Down in the valley, amid the scrum of men, it was possible to see a lengthy shield wall just about holding together against cavalry charges that repeatedly challenged it.

"It's just a mess," said Maddie.

"We have to get closer if we want to see what happened to Harold," said Astrid.

Shields raised, they moved away from the sodden patch of land and proceeded towards the edge of the fighting.

"Hoy!" came a yell.

Two men wearing little armour were walking up towards them, carrying a wounded man between them on a makeshift stretcher. The two men were streaked with dirt and blood, but seemed otherwise unscathed.

One beckoned them over. "Get down there! Leofwine is hurt!"

The meaning was clear. They were to follow. Maddie looked back for signs of Alice, but she had gone.

"I guess we're doing this?" she said to Astrid. "We're fetching bodies or wounded?"

"I imagine it will depend upon how important they are," said Astrid.

The two men had dropped off the man they were carrying. The undignified manner in which he was deposited did not bode well for his chances.

"There's tents up there through the trees," said Astrid, pointing. "Maybe the merely wounded get taken up there."

They followed the two men back towards the battle. They lifted their shields again as a flurry of arrows came in.

"We should have worked on our upper body strength," Astrid puffed. "This is intolerable."

"It's war!" Maddie shouted.

"Well, I don't approve!"

They drew closer to the fighting – the thump of metal on wood, the yelling, the screaming – picking their way between bodies, some of them clearly not dead yet. The men were leading them on, deeper.

"We could just jump back," hissed Astrid. "This isn't safe."

Maddie was struck by a sudden and deep feeling of

despair. This was just one moment in history, and it was full of death and suffering. And history was a long succession of such moments. Maddie felt herself caught between Alice and Astrid: one woman who would, given the chance, save every wounded human or animal in history, and one who currently wanted to flee from the horrors as swiftly as possible. Faced with all this suffering the options available ranged from the unpalatable to the futile. She felt sick.

Then they were signalled to stop. The stretcher in front of them was set down beside a man who, beneath the universal coating of filth, was wearing much more finely made garments. He had a large wound in his side. They were directed to retrieve another man further along, clearly also a man of importance. His arm was bleeding severely and he was unconscious.

"Faster!" called a robust, middle-aged man on horseback. Maddie hadn't noticed him as they'd been so focussed on the ground. "Take him to safety!"

The one on horseback seemed to be almost untouched by the muck coating everyone else. He was at the head of a ragged body of horsemen, two of them carrying army standards.

"Take Ulf to safety!" he ordered.

They loaded the injured man onto their cobbled-together stretcher.

"Astrid! Astrid! Is that Harold?" hissed Maddie.

"I shall return, cuz!" the man on the stretcher croaked, stretching out his one good arm.

"It is Harold," breathed Astrid and looked back at the horseman. For a moment, she seemed to forget to be afraid.

There was the quietest of sighs, and abruptly Alice was back with them. She had her shield in one hand and a massive modern paramedic's satchel slung over her shoulder.

"Good God in heaven!" yelled Harold, seeing the woman appear before him. His horse skittered in alarm.

"Arrows!" someone hollered.

Alice pressed forward to Maddie and Astrid, holding her shield high, doing her best to cover them all. Maddie crouched to get herself as much under the shelter as possible.

Astrid cupped her hands. "Harold! Harold! Don't look up!"

The king, trying to control his horse, frowned at Astrid, then Maddie saw him look instinctively skywards.

The inevitable happened.

Harold didn't even make a sound as he tumbled from his horse.

Astrid looked at Maddie, stricken with shock.

Maddie grimaced. "Shall we run now?" she suggested, trying very hard not sound sarcastic.

The three of them, two bearing the injured noble and one holding a shield above them all, ran from the battlefield as fast as they could.

15

T hey didn't stop running until they were by the pool close to where they had first arrived. Maddie and Astrid deposited the injured man on the grass.

"Oh, this is awful," said Astrid.

Alice couldn't be sure if the comment was directed at her own sore and aching body, the overall pointlessness of war or, as it clearly seemed to Alice, the fact that Astrid herself had caused King Harold to get shot in the eye.

Alice put such questions aside and knelt beside the injured man. "Hello, I'm Alice. I'm going to dress your wounds. What's your name?"

"This is Ulf," said Maddie, collapsing on the ground, exhausted.

Alice worked swiftly, unpackaging bandages and creams and materials from the bag she'd brought on her return journey. There was needle and thread. She washed the man's arm with a bottle of sterilised water, removing the jewelled bracelet on his wrist to do so, then bent to sew his wound together again. The man didn't flinch once.

"You've got a paramedic's bag," said Maddie eventually.

"I have," said Alice. "Little first aid kits didn't seem enough."

"Where did you get a paramedic's bag?"

"Stole it off a paramedic."

"Makes sense."

Astrid seemed to come back from whatever mortified corner of her mind she'd been dwelling in for the last few minutes. "And you changed," she said. "Your clothes are clean."

"We're time travellers," said Alice. "We've got time to do all the things."

"So—" said Maddie in a very careful voice "—we know the answer to the pub quiz question now."

Alice paused in her bandaging of Ulf's arm to look at Astrid.

"No," Astrid declared.

"No?"

"We've changed history. Yes. Harold has now died from an arrow to the eye. Who knows what would have happened if—" She shut her eyes.

"Regretting telling him not to look up?" Maddie suggested.

Astrid sighed.

"She'll be fine in a few minutes. What did you do with the horse by the way?"

Alice gestured in no real direction at all and put some

finishing touches onto Ulf's arm. "Rest up here for a little while. You've lost a lot of blood, so don't get up."

She steered Maddie and Astrid away from the stretcher and the three of them huddled together to exchange whispers.

"Are you saying we got what we came here for?" asked Alice. "We know what happened?"

"Yes. It's probably time to go home now," said Astrid weakly.

Alice held onto the others and with one final look at the injured Ulf, they jumped, landing together in Astrid's living room.

Alice looked at her two fellow travellers. They were all shattered, and splattered feet to necks in mud.

"How long were we actually there?" said Maddie, her voice hollow.

"An hour?" suggested Astrid, numbly.

Maddie nodded. "Let's not go back there again."

"No." Astrid considered herself. "I'm going to get a shower."

She came back downstairs half an hour later, her male clothes discarded and her stuck on facial hair washed away.

Maddie's phone buzzed. She looked at it. "Voicemail."

"Alice, I would like to ask you something," said Astrid, a very different tone in her voice now.

Alice had a fair idea what that tone of voice actually meant.

"Cup of tea?" she said with forced cheer and hurried into the kitchen. She pulled down the roller blind on the window overlooking the back garden and made a big clattering show of filling the kettle. Her mind had jumped to the conclusion that if she made a lot of noise, she wouldn't be able to hear what Astrid said next.

"There I was," said Astrid, "getting dried after what I can only describe as the most wonderful shower I've taken since the Norman era, when I happened to look out of my bedroom window at the boggy morass your cow had made of my back garden, and what did I happen—"

"Er, guys," said Maddie, coming into the kitchen with her phone. "I think you ought to—"

"And what did I happen to see?" demanded Astrid, unwilling to be interrupted.

"Guys..." insisted Maddie.

Astrid reached over and released the roller blind. It shot up and revealed both cow and horse now resident in the garden. The two beasts, side by side, gazed through the window at the women.

"Oh," said Maddie. "Oh, that's not good."

Astrid flung out an angry arm. "Why? I mean why?!"

"I had nowhere else to take them!" said Alice, feeling both a wretchedness at upsetting her host and a heated need to offer these creatures protection.

"You had everywhere to take them!" said Astrid. "Literally anywhere in the world. And at any time! That's everywhere multiplied by every ... when. Here. In my garden. At this moment. This was not the place to put them. A Stuart cow and a Norman horse! Are we doing a time-travel pet rescue centre? Going to get a Tudor goat and a Victorian guinea pig next, huh?!"

"Look, I said I'm sorry..." said Alice.

"You said no such thing!" said Astrid.

"Then I'm sorry, Mistress Boucher."

"Oh! Don't you come the naïve little girl from the past with me! Mistress Boucher indeed!"

"Guys! Guys!" said Maddie, cutting through them. "I *really* think you need to listen to this." She thrust the phone between them and touched an icon.

"*You have one message,*" said a robot lady's voice, then the next voice was Maddie's own. It spoke in a clear, bright and entirely false tone. "*Hi there. I borrowed the inspector guy's phone because mine is 'low on juice'. You've probably not realised what time it is. Maybe even not noticed what date it is. I'm going to be seeing you in a bit, but I've got to accompany this inspector to check on someone allegedly keeping a cow and a horse in her back garden. Can you imagine—?*"

"*Oh, the things I've seen,*" drawled a man's voice on the recording. Alice realised Maddie was talking while in a vehicle with this inspector character.

"*—Anyway, it'll be a big fine if the inspector finds they're keeping animals illegally,*" said Maddie on the phone. "*I'm going to be doing the inspection at two p.m. and I'll guess I'll see you not long after. See you soon!*"

The message ended.

Alice looked at the clock on the wall. "It is half past one."

Maddie was holding up her phone. "We didn't quite hit our return target. We've come back five days after we left."

"And now the council inspector is coming to check on my livestock," fumed Astrid.

"And *I'm* coming with him," said Maddie.

"Okay, okay," said Alice. "I'm sure there's something we can do."

"Bloody right there is," said Astrid. "You can start thinking about how you can get me a thousand pounds to pay off that fine."

There was a ring of the doorbell. Alice looked at the clock again. "But it's not two o'clock yet," she said.

"Do not ask for whom the bell tolls," Astrid scowled and stormed to the door.

16

Astrid wrenched her front door open. The man on the doorstep was not a council inspector. It was Brian bloody Leadcock. He stood on her doorstep, far too close to her door, a slight smile just underneath that stupid bristly grey moustache of his.

"Yes?" she said curtly.

"Astrid," he said smoothly. "So glad I caught you while you were in. I've been round several times this week but I think you must have been away. Go somewhere nice?"

"I'm very busy, Brian," she said. "I don't have time to talk."

"It won't take a moment."

"I doubt that," she said, then, because he didn't look like he was about to leave, added, "What is it then? Spit it out."

"It's about your delivery man."

She gave him a deliberately blank look. "What delivery man?"

His hand swept out to take in her driveway. "The builder's

merchant or whatever. Nearly knocked down the ornamental gate post as he backed up to your house."

"I have no idea what you're talking about, Brian. And frankly I don't care."

"The issue here is that he left all his muck all over the path and the road. I had to get out my SPX3000 power washer and clean up. Glenn Coleman came out offering to use his Karcher K5, which was just silly. The SPX has got a higher pressure of two-thousand-and-thirty PSI, outperforming the Karcher K5 Premium with its mere two thousand PSI. The SPX just packs more punch. A no-brainer, really."

Astrid stared at him.

"I'm talking about power washers," said Brian.

"I gather," said Astrid. "I just don't understand why you think I'd give a shit."

"Astrid!"

"And I don't know anything about a delivery lorry or muck on the road. And I really don't care. We're just ants on the surface of a dying world in a huge and indifferent universe and you think I give a fucking shit about which pressure washer has the highest PSI. Now, you've said your piece. Could you possibly fuck off now? I've got things to deal with."

"Oh, yes," said Brian. "The council inspector is coming round today, isn't he?" The smile on his face, momentarily wiped off by her vulgarity, returned in force. "My friend, Michael Goole at the council, was good enough to give me a heads up." He frowned. "Will he issue a ticket, like a traffic warden, I wonder? Slap it on old Bessie back there." He laughed at his own mental image.

His presence – his very existence – was sapping energy from her soul. "I'm sure I told you to fuck off," she said. "And if you don't, I'll be tempted to do to you what I did to King Harold."

"Pardon?"

She was about to slam the door in his face when a long car up drew up outside the front of the house. The man who got out wore a sensible coat, wellington boots, and an official looking ID card on a lanyard.

"No," said Astrid. "This is not—" She looked at her watch. "This is not two o'clock."

The woman who got out of the passenger side of the car was Maddie Waites, dressed entirely differently to earlier. Astrid noted once again that Maddie didn't seem to differentiate between her workwear and her slovenly casual wear.

"Good afternoon, Ms Boucher," said Maddie in a carefully formal voice.

The man approached. Brian Leadcock stepped aside to give him room and observe the spectacle.

The council inspector introduced himself and entered into a long spiel that he'd clearly memorised.

"Yes, yes, yes," said Astrid. "You've come to inflict yourself upon me and to pry into what I do on my own private property. You want to see the cow, don't you?"

"Alleged cow," said Maddie unnecessarily.

"The smells it's been creating are something awful," offered Brian.

"Shut up, Brian," said Astrid. "Well, there's no point putting off the inevitable, is there?" She stepped out of the front door and walked them round to the rear of the house.

"Was the cow meant to be a pet?" asked the inspector in a friendly and conversational manner.

"What?" said Astrid.

"Or were you keeping it for milk, for example."

Astrid was about to point out that she wasn't the one who'd put the cow in the garden in the first place, and she wasn't responsible for the horse they'd find there either, when she rounded the corner and stopped in surprise.

"Oh," said the inspector.

There was no cow in the garden. There was no horse either for that matter. Far more mystifying in its own way, there was no sign that the cow had ever been there. Over the past week or more Teasel had churned up the perfectly ordinary lawn into a quagmire to match the muddy battlefield at Hastings. But now, in front of them all, was a fresh green lawn. Astrid could see the lines between the rolls of new turf that had been laid, but as lawns went, it was not half bad.

"Where's the cow?" said Brian, who had followed them round.

"What cow?" said Maddie.

He strode onto the lawn. "It was here. It was here this morning. I saw."

"Peering over people's fences, sir?" The inspector, straight-faced, made a show of looking round the small garden, in case there might be a cow hiding behind a stunted shrub or next to the garden waste bin.

"Is this it?" asked Maddie, pointing to a rough terracotta planter in the shape of an amiable and cartoonish cow.

"Huge cow!" said Brian, in spluttering disbelief.

Astrid didn't understand, but she would happily make capital from the incident while she could. "I don't suppose there's a finable offence for wasting council inspectors' time, is there?" she asked.

The inspector gave her a small, polite smile. "You have a very nice garden, Ms Boucher." He looked to Maddie.

"Yes," she agreed. "Onto the next one?"

The two council employees walked back round the front of the house.

Astrid turned to Brian. "Now get the fuck out of my garden," she said.

Struggling for a retort but currently speechless, Brian retreated.

Maddie and the inspector were already getting back into the car. Brian seemed unable to process that his moment of schadenfreude had been stolen from him and hovered at the edge of her driveway.

"All the way off my property, you dull and horrible little man, before I set the cow on you," said Astrid and went back inside.

Alice was in the living room, cleaned and changed after their trip to Norman England. Astrid gave her a questioning look.

"Ta dah!" said Alice, giving her enthusiastic jazz hands.

Astrid pointed at the garden. "You?"

"Me and Maddie."

"But that was like all in five minutes."

Alice nodded in hearty agreement. "It did take some doing. We jumped Teasel and Norman away."

"Norman the horse?"

"It's a good name."

"She was a female horse."

"Norman's a good name," insisted Alice. "And then we went back a week and purchased some turf. We had it delivered the other day."

"The delivery lorry he was moaning about," said Astrid, understanding.

"It comes in these great little rolls, like rugs. I've never seen that before. We had it stored round the far corner."

"You had it rolled out in ten minutes?"

"We might have had to jump back and forth a bit. Met ourselves coming back a couple of times, but..."

"And the pottery cow?"

"Thought you'd appreciate the joke."

Astrid, who was rarely in the mood for jokes, gave a thin-lipped acknowledgement that it had been worth seeing the look on Brian Leadcock's face when the only cow to be found in the garden was made from terracotta.

"But how did you afford it? To turf a new garden— You didn't steal it, did you?"

Alice's expression was now somewhat contrite. "Well..." she began hesitantly, "you know how I tended to that man's wounds on the battlefield?"

"Yes?"

"I might have slipped off his gold bracelet. It has these lovely garnets set into it."

"Oh."

"And Maddie and I discovered that if you look hard enough, even in a town like Wirkswell, you can find a pawnbroker who'll give you several hundred pounds for a thousand year old gold bracelet. And we could even use some of it to pay the people up at the pony trekking place to let us put Teasel and Norman in a paddock." Alice dug into the back pocket of her jeans. She pulled out a folded wad of cash. "There's not much left but..." She held the cash out to Astrid. "Consider it rent?"

Astrid took it. She was not a woman given to strong emotions, but she felt something warm and heartening – and not necessarily very pleasant – stirring inside her.

"You are a surprising young woman, sometimes," she said.

"I'm learning," said Alice.

17

M addie sat down at her office desk and considered the overflowing pile of work that still filled her physical in-tray. Managing to do her own job while continuing to take on the work of the flooded out environmental team necessitated the acceptance that her workload would never ease, that the in-tray would never be empty. Even though the work was never-ending, the week had turned out well. The plan to rehouse two large mammals and returf Astrid's garden had paid off. It had felt like a considerable effort to avoid a council fine, but there had been a challenge and neatness to it that made it all seem worthwhile.

On top of that, there would be no further conflict between Astrid and the council, nor inner conflict between Maddie's work life and personal life.

The phone on her desk rang. She picked up. "Maddie

Waites. Parks and Amenities and Environmental Services and Surprising Feats of Magic."

"Is that Maddie Waites?" came a woman's voice.

"Yes. The one and only."

"I'm Phillipa Brown, PA to the mayoral office. The mayor wondered if he could have a moment of your time."

"The mayor?"

Maddie knew that Wirkswell had a mayor. It had a town council, and the leader of that council would, she guessed, be given the honorific title of mayor. But even though she worked for the council, Maddie had never given much thought to the people who notionally sat at the top of it. She understood, and mostly rejected, the idea that the town councillors were in charge of things. To her mind, it seemed quite unfair and silly that the people who worked their entire lives doing the important business of maintaining the streetlights, the bin collections, the libraries, the parks and all the things that kept a small town ticking over, should have to pay any attention to amateurs who were only in charge because they won a popular vote every couple of years. Councillors were not, in her mind, of any significance or consequence.

Maddie had never met the mayor, had no desire to, and struggled to reconcile the idea that the existence of a mayor had any relevance to her job.

"Yes," said the PA, Phillipa Brown. *"Now, if you're available. We're on the third floor."*

"Yeah. Sure." She locked her computer and stood. "Called to the mayor's office," she told her co-workers.

"Have you been a bad girl?" said one. Her wild eyebrow waggles seemed to think her comment was wittier than it truly was.

"If I'm not back in an hour, please preserve my workspace as a shrine to my memory," said Maddie and went in search of the mayor.

The stairs leading up to the third floor were dark and smelled of mould. There was a bucket in the centre of the upper corridor to catch drips of water still coming through the ceiling. The door to Environmental Services had a *Do Not Enter* notice taped to it.

Maddie sidestepped the bucket and proceeded down the corridor. The light clacking of a keyboard drew her to an open door at the far end. The water leakage had not spread to this part of the building. There was a polished gleam to the dark floorboard, and the walls were dotted with photographs of functions, festivals and general backslappery from a hundred years of the council.

A woman in a frilly and old-fashioned blouse sat at a desk beyond the open door.

"Maddie Waites?" said Phillipa Brown PA.

"That's me."

Phillipa Brown PA gestured to the open door and the office beyond.

"Through here?" said Maddie.

"Through there."

A peculiar unease had settled on Maddie. Maybe it was gentle opulence of this little corner of this building. Whatever it was, she wished she'd come to work this morning in something other than her usual rock band T-shirt and jeans.

Telling herself not to be silly, she stepped forward into the mayor's office. The man himself sat behind a wide desk beneath a sealed up chimney breast. Above the chimney breast hung a ceremonial shield and a sword. An actual sword and shield. Maddie knew some cosplayers and LARPers who would sell their mums for a sword and shield like that.

The mayor hadn't noticed her enter. He was bent over a document, poring over it with a fountain pen in hand, ready to jot amendments.

Maddie cleared her throat.

"With you in a moment," he said. "Just need to dot some 'i's and cross some 't's. Maddie Waites waits."

He took a full ten seconds to get to the bottom of the page, during which there wasn't even the ticking of a clock to break the silence, then he looked up.

For half a second, Maddie thought she must have met the mayor before because she recognised his face. Then, with a stomach flip, she realised she had seen the man before. Twice.

She had seen his face in a photo Astrid had taken in seventeen hundred and something. She had seen his face herself in flickering firelight a hundred years earlier. The beards had been different on those occasions and now it was entirely gone, but it was exactly the same man.

"Master Burnleigh—" she coughed in surprise.

He smiled pleasantly. "Mister Burnley was my dad. I'm Nate. Nate Burnley. Or Mr Mayor if you must."

He held out a hand to shake. Maddie numbly took it.

"Now," he said, indicating for her to sit, "you really must tell me all about this business with the entirely imaginary cow. It sounds like quite an adventure."

18

Astrid discovered that during their leaping about through time, while she'd been distracted at the front door, Maddie and Alice hadn't only rehomed a cow and returfed a lawn, but also had time to order and eat a takeaway (the remains of which were in Astrid's bin), put on the dishwasher (stacking the cups in entirely the wrong way) and stick on a load of washing (foolishly bunging whites and colours in together on far too high a temperature). Despite their poor approach to household chores, it was nice that Astrid was soon folding the now-clean 'man' clothes she'd been trying out for much of the week.

Alice was in the living room, doodling ideas in a notepad. "You know that Skid is still alive," she said.

"Yes?" said Astrid, small pile of clothes in her hand.

"Calls himself James. Says he's turning his life around."

"Yes."

"We actually succeeded there."

"We did. We should be proud."

"We can permanently change history."

Astrid pressed her lips together in thought. "So, on the face of it, I was the reason for King Harold getting killed by an arrow in his eye."

"You were."

"It reminds me somewhat of Skid. We saved him once and he found another way to get killed. Maybe there's some inevitability to our universe. Regardless of my actions, it *is* possible that Harold was always going to be shot in the eye."

"But we saved Skid," said Alice.

Astrid nodded. "And you are thinking that you can go back and save your Merrial?"

Alice flinched. Astrid had guessed right.

"Perhaps we should not drive ourselves insane thinking about what could have been," said Astrid, "and simply accept things as they are. I didn't want Harold to get an arrow in the eye but he did."

Alice peered at her. "You didn't want him to get an arrow in the eye because you wanted him to live? Or because you wanted to be right about the answer to the pub quiz?"

Astrid wasn't going to dignify that with an answer, so took the pile of clothes upstairs.

In the tiny rear room she looked for the box from where she'd got the men's clothes in the first place, couldn't recall which of them it might have been, so neatly placed them in the nearest. In the box of old children's books, she saw the copy of *Meet the Cavemen!* by Ricardo Bushrat.

With a grunt of nostalgia, she took it out again and

flicked through. There truly was something sweet about the warmth and effort with which older book illustrations were—

She stopped. The book was open at the page of ancient people exploring the vast woodlands of prehistoric Europe, and Astrid immediately realised she had seen that scene before. Not only seen it: she'd stood in it.

Gripped with more curiosity and determination than caution, Astrid focused her mind and jumped. She stood, as she had done before, in the knee high grass beneath a clear morning sky. Far down the slope of this hillside was the edge of a forest far denser and greater than any that could be found in modern Britain. The wind and the open sky once again gave her the sense that this was a world far removed from the crowded and hurried world she had come from. This was a world that was able to open its lungs and just breathe...

She looked at the illustration in the book. It was not just a similar landscape, it was *this* landscape. That tussocky hillock there. That broken little tree down there. As she looked, there was some movement at the edge of the distant wood. Short biped figures.

She looked at the illustration once more before closing the book to look afresh at the cover.

"Ricardo Bushrat," she whispered. "How the hell is this possible?"

ABOUT THE AUTHORS

Heide Goody lives in North Warwickshire with her family and pets. Iain Grant lives in South Birmingham with his family and pets.

They are both married but not to each other.

Clovenhoof

Getting fired can ruin a day...

...especially when you were the Prince of Hell.

Will Satan survive in English suburbia?

Corporate life can be a soul draining experience, especially when the industry is Hell, and you're Lucifer. It isn't all torture and brimstone, though, for the Prince of Darkness, he's got an unhappy Board of Directors.

The numbers look bad.

They want him out.

Then came the corporate coup.

Banished to mortal earth as Jeremy Clovenhoof, Lucifer is going through a mid-immortality crisis of biblical proportion. Maybe if he just tries to blend in, it won't be so bad.

He's wrong.

If it isn't the murder, cannibalism, and armed robbery of everyday life in Birmingham, it's the fact that his heavy metal band isn't getting the respect it deserves, that's dampening his mood.

And the archangel Michael constantly snooping on him, doesn't help.

If you enjoy clever writing, then you'll adore this satirical tour de force, because a good laugh can make you have sympathy for the devil.

Get it now.

Clovenhoof

Oddjobs

Unstoppable horrors from beyond are poised to invade and literally create Hell on Earth.

It's the end of the world as we know it, but someone still needs to do the paperwork.

Morag Murray works for the secret government organisation responsible for making sure the apocalypse goes as smoothly and as quietly as possible.

Trouble is, Morag's got a temper problem and, after angering the wrong alien god, she's been sent to another city where she won't cause so much trouble.

But Morag's got her work cut out for her. She has to deal with a man-eating starfish, solve a supernatural murder and, if she's got time, prevent her own inevitable death.

If you like The Laundry Files, The Chronicles of St Mary's or Men in Black, you'll love the Oddjobs series."If Jodi Taylor wrote a Laundry Files novel set it in Birmingham... A hilarious dose of bleak existential despair. With added tentacles! And bureaucracy!"
– Charles Stross, author of The Laundry Files series.

Oddjobs

Printed in Great Britain
by Amazon

36411705R00073